Although the setting and telling of the story are utterly
timeless, it's a narrative that feels completely relevant
for the children who will read it today. As world events
can seem bleak and threatening, what could speak
louder than a story like this—that shows us the power
of hope, of resilience, and of belief that every one of us
can always make a difference.

My wish as you read *The House of Light* is that it will seep
into your heart the way it has done into mine—and that
it will carry its message of light and hope far and wide.

Liz Cross
Head of Children's Publishing, OUP

Praise for To the Edge of the World

'Absolutely swept away by Julia Green's new book *To the Edge of the World* . . . a wonderful read.'
Gill Lewis

'A quietly lovely book full of birds and boats and faraway places. It reminded me of the joy of exploration, and why I love the Scottish Isles.'
Sally Nicholls

'Just finished Julia's wonderful story and, as I expected, absolutely adored it. It's such a lovely story of facing our fears and daring to be different. Loved the world she's created—the nature imagery, the sea, the family dynamics—definitely the work of an exceptional writer! I think Django is fast becoming my favourite fictional dog!'
Emma Carroll

'This story about identity, friendship and becoming yourself has everything: real adventure, real danger all set in a real place, with the wonder of a magical realm, plus an irresistible dog! A story as clear and powerful as an Atlantic wave.'
Nicola Davies

For David

OXFORD
UNIVERSITY PRESS

Great Clarendon Street, Oxford OX2 6DP

Oxford University Press is a department of the University of Oxford.
It furthers the University's objective of excellence in research, scholarship,
and education by publishing worldwide. Oxford is a registered trade mark
of Oxford University Press in the UK and in certain other countries

British Library Cataloguing in Publication Data

Data available

ISBN: 978-01-9277156-8

1 3 5 7 9 10 8 6 4 2

Printed in Great Britain

Paper used in the production of this book is a natural,
recyclable product made from wood grown in sustainable forests.
The manufacturing process conforms to the environmental
regulations of the country of origin.

THE
HOUSE
OF
LIGHT

Julia Green

OXFORD
UNIVERSITY PRESS

The Discovery

The beach smelled of fish today. The sea was a deep navy blue. It was funny how it changed all the time. Bonnie wrinkled her nose. Yes, fish, and salt, and something else, like burnt toast. Maybe someone had lit a fire, only the beach was empty, so that couldn't be it. She jumped from the last bit of dune path down onto the sand. The tide was going out, and the wind from the north. It blew the pale, dry sand over the darker damp sand like streams of smoke. Her ears ached with cold. She turned her coat collar up and tucked her hair inside.

No one else was fool enough to walk on a freezing windy beach on a January morning. Well, everyone was in school, most likely. Which is where she should have been, only she'd had enough of being bored out of her mind, and shouted at, and teased for being different, and when she'd told Granda she wasn't going, not today and not ever again, he had not said anything at all. He'd carried on with his work as if he hadn't heard her. Maybe he hadn't. But she'd soon had enough of sitting in the dark house, and so she'd run down the lane and over the field to the path through the sand dunes, and here she was. She'd brought the big metal bucket, in case there was stuff to take home, stuff the sea brought in with each new tide. She plonked it down at the top of the beach near the Border Notice and the concrete blocks, big ugly things which had been put there to stop tanks invading from the sea in some old war, years and years ago.

A flock of small brown-and-white birds took off with a whirr of wings as she got closer to the water's edge. She screwed up her eyes to look closely: sanderlings, winter plumage, juveniles—which meant last year's babies, in their first winter feathers. Further out, a bigger bird with a long curved beak searched for food in the pools on the flat rocks newly exposed by the retreating tide. Curlew. It flew off, too, as she stepped carefully over the slippery weed on the rocks.

Further out to sea, a flotilla of small islands was part of the same seam of rock called the Whin Sill. Bonnie loved Granda's stories about the islands, about the people who once lived there and tended special houses of light to warn passing ships of the rocks, and rescued shipwrecked fisherfolk, and about ghosts and strange birds that only came at night. He said there were more than twenty-five islands at low tide, but only one big enough to live on. If the light was right, on the clearest days, you could sometimes glimpse the islands glimmering on the horizon, coming and going as the light shifted so that Bonnie wondered if they were really there at all. It was too far and too dangerous to go there, and in any case they didn't have a boat. Not any more.

The waves raced to the shore, chasing each other, their white crests curling over and spreading out into lacy foam, fine tendrils whipped behind by the wind like hair, like a horse's mane.

Enough daydreaming, Bonnie! Work to be done! Bonnie heard Granda's voice as clear as if he were right at her side.

She retraced her steps back along the ridge of rocks onto the sand and ran along the tideline hunting for useful things washed up. There was always plastic stuff, but that wasn't good for much. It was usually cracked and smelly and you could get poisoned by the liquids that had once been stored inside. Wood was more rare and precious. Sometimes she found bits of sea coal, and that made Granda happy. Once it had dried out it made the fire blaze hot and bright. Bonnie found a length of fishing net that could be mended. Good. And two old leather shoes, not matching and too big for Bonnie, but they could be dried and traded or turned into something else. There were shells aplenty, which was a good sign. It meant that the sea was recovering, getting back to health after the long time of waste and spoil.

She went back for the bucket, and dumped the net and the old shoes, ready to take back home later. Food harvest, next. She perched on the Whin Sill, peering into pools, careful not to let her shadow fall across the water and scare off everything alive. She pulled up the sticky sea-flowers that were actually creatures even though they looked like plants—never more than one clump from each pool; you must always leave enough behind—and picked green crabs from under pebbles, and put them in the bucket. She found fresh green edible sea-leaves, and the pink seaweed that tasted good in soup. She scooped up small shrimpy things, and put them into the bucket with enough seawater to keep them fresh. Each time, she said thank you, and sorry, for the life taken.

Her hands were frozen. She put the bucket down on the sand, and shoved her hands deep in her coat pockets to warm them. She straightened up and stretched her spine out, and there—just for a second—a flicker of movement up in the dunes startled her. Was someone there? She waited, but nothing moved. Perhaps it had just been wind blowing the dune grass. Or the shadow of a bird.

The bank of tall dunes at the top of the beach was high and deep just here. Deep rutted paths of sand ran between massive clumps of dune grass. Children played there sometimes—hide-and-seek, and tag—and sometimes on summer evenings couples came to lie together in the sun, out of the wind, out of view. The dune grass was yellow and gold, like hair.

A thin line of sunlight pierced the mass of grey cloud over the land.

Bonnie studied the line of the dunes again.

Was there something there?

She could make out the grey shape of something. Perhaps it was part of a dead tree washed up ages ago and buried in the sand for months, and now the wind had shifted the sand and unburied it again. It might be big and strong enough to make something new for the house. Shelves for her room. A new bed, even.

Bonnie went closer. Her boots sank in the soft dry sand.

It was not a tree.

Her heart gave a little skip.

It was the upturned hull of a wooden boat.

Boat

Bonnie ran her hands over the sea-weathered wood. Some of the planks—the ones that would have been underwater when the boat was at sea—were encrusted with barnacles and the scribbly lines of sea snail tracks. With her coat sleeve she brushed away the rest of the sand.

The wood was grey and old but the boat looked almost seaworthy—just a few damaged planks needed mending and caulking with pitch. She tried to lift it, but it was much too heavy, wedged deep in sand. She shoved it hard, and heard the drip drip of water underneath. Water? As if the boat had recently been in the sea, not washed up months or years ago and buried in the sand until today.

How could she carry it home by herself, when it was so heavy, and so wedged down? But if she didn't, if she left it here while she went to fetch Granda, someone else might find it and claim it as theirs, when it was she, Bonnie, who was the rightful owner. She'd found it first.

If she could turn it the other way up maybe she could slide it over the soft dry sand and up the path at least as far as the field, and she could hide it there in the hawthorn hedge, until she could come back with Granda.

A shadow flew over her mind when she thought of Granda, because there had once been a boat, a beautiful wooden boat a bit like this one, but bigger, and the boat had carried away the person Granda cared most about in the world—except Bonnie, of course. His daughter Frances, who was Bonnie's mam. This boat might bring back sad memories for Granda. Perhaps she should keep it a secret, for now.

Bonnie had been just a toddler when her mam had gone, and she did not remember anything about her. There was one small photo of her mam as a girl, in a silver frame on Granda's bedside table. Bonnie's life had always been just her and Granda. She had never known anything else.

'You are my consolation and my salvation, Bonnie,' Granda would say. 'My pearl beyond price.' She didn't really know what he meant but she knew that it was a good thing: he loved her deeply and wanted her to be happy.

Bonnie shoved the boat one more time with all her weight. It still wouldn't budge. Already the sky was getting dark, massive grey clouds looming up over the land behind the beach, and the chill in the air was freezing her hands and cheeks. If she couldn't move it, then no one else could either, she reasoned. And snow was on the way, Granda had said so last night. Surely no one would come down to the beach now. She'd have to trust that her boat would still be here in the morning.

Bonnie turned her back on the boat and trudged through the soft dry sand at the top of the beach in the shelter of the dunes. She worked out a plan as she walked, the cold metal bucket banging into her legs. She could bring ropes, and find a way to haul the boat back by herself. If the snow was deep enough she could slide the boat all the way up the lane, like a sledge, and hide it in one of the outhouses out of sight, until the time seemed right to tell Granda about the treasure she had found.

It was meant for her, she was suddenly sure of it. A message, and a gift.

The boat was an invitation, calling her out into the world. There was more than her small house and the village where she'd lived her whole life. Wide oceans; lands to explore.

A bit further along, she found the remains of a fire. She kicked the charred sticks and ash and wondered who had made it, and how long ago. She glanced back at the boat. The dunes near it looked as if they were moving, part of some big living creature, but it was just the wind rattling the grass. She walked on. It was much too cold to stand still for long.

Her arm ached. She swapped the bucket over to her other hand. She remembered to pick up the shoes and the bundle of old fishing net she'd left near the concrete blocks, and shoved them under her arm. She glanced back along the beach. She could make out the trail of her footsteps disappearing into the distance, but she couldn't see the boat any longer. Good; that meant no one else would be able to, either.

The first flurry of sleet arrived on a gust of wind. It stung her cheeks.

Bonnie hurried on home.

It seemed strange to see snow settling on the dune grass, on sand. Already the sleet was turning to thick, soft flakes the size of a baby's fist. Snow was another good sign, because snow was what was supposed to come in winter, and for many years there had been none. And the bitter cold was good, because it killed off the bugs and germs that made people ill and plants diseased. But Bonnie wished her coat were thicker and longer. She was growing out of the clothes she'd had for years, which once had been much too big. Where were new ones going to come from?

She pulled her coat hood up for the millionth time. Her other hand was half frozen against the bucket handle. It was a relief to get to the shelter of the hawthorn hedge that ran the length of the field and then the lane. The snow was falling more slowly now, as if it was going to take its own time.

Ahead she saw the faint light at the window of the first house. Some of the village houses had electric from the wind-powered generator. She kept her head down as she skirted the village. She took the footpath that ran behind the old ruined church and the disused public house, and cut across the small field with its copse of pine trees. The air smelled of wood smoke, which meant she was almost home.

For a moment the snow stopped falling, and in the sudden stillness the sky seemed to lighten. A skein of pink-footed geese flew over her, high in the cold air, calling and honking to each other. It was a lonely sound that seemed to fill her with longing, though why or for what she could not say. She stopped to watch them. The bird out front dropped back and another took its place. They flew in a V shape because that was the most efficient way, she supposed. And so they took turns, since that was the most tiring position, out front, navigating the way for the others. It was a miracle how they knew where to go. They travelled thousands of miles. The geese must have known about the cold coming, and so they were flying south, just in front of the snowstorm.

Bonnie hurried on. She pushed the garden gate open, stomped her snowy boots on the path up to the back door and went inside the house. She left her boots and the net and the bucket on the stone-flagged floor in the kitchen.

'Granda?' she called into the dark house. 'The geese are here!'

Her voice echoed through the house. Granda didn't answer. He was probably outside, shutting up the hens for the night. Bonnie shivered. The house was colder than usual. Had he let the fire die out?

She went back to the kitchen and lifted the heavy lid on the range. The fire inside was nothing but a smoulder of embers. It wasn't like Granda to let it go so low. The basket of logs was empty, too. She'd have to get more logs from the woodpile outside in the shed, and that meant putting her boots back on.

The wind snatched the door back the moment she opened it, and snow whirled inside. Bonnie pulled her hood up. She put the basket on her hip and staggered across the yard to the shed. Everything was raw and damp and icy. The metal latch hurt her fingers. The logs scraped the skin on her hands when she lifted them from the pile and threw them into the basket. She heard something scuttling away, claws scratching the rough floor—a rat, most likely—and had to force herself to carry on filling the basket. On the way back across the yard she peered into the snowy darkness to see if Granda was on his way back from the hen shed, but it was impossible to make out anything.

She slammed the door behind her as she went inside. She shoved the basket back into place and put two logs onto the stove fire. Her boots left a trail of puddles. She took them off and hung her coat on the pegs on the door.

Bonnie leant against the stove to warm herself up. There was barely enough heat. She lit the lamp on the ceiling hook and put another log on the fire but it was damp and made the fire steam and spit. She dragged a chair over to the stove and settled down.

She thought about the geese. How far would they go tonight? Maybe they'd stop at the lake, and she would get the chance to watch them. One year, the geese had stopped to feed on the field, and she had loved to sit quietly to watch them, to listen to the way they talked to each other. She loved the whoosh of their wings when they all took flight together, wheeling up and away into the sky. The geese seemed like a promise of something.

She imagined the snow settling on the upside-down boat. When the weather was better, when spring came, she could row herself out to the islands, and see for herself the stone house where once they had kept a light burning every night. Maybe the walled garden was still there, like in Granda's stories, and she could catch the deepwater fish that were not poisoned and were safe to eat.

She shivered.

A school inspector had announced that children must not go near the sea. 'It is too dangerous. The islands are poisoned with sickness and death. You must keep away from such terrible places.'

But that wasn't true, was it?

Granda had been furious when she told him. 'Made-up, superstitious nonsense! Lies and fear-mongering. Take no notice, Bonnie.'

She'd fetch the boat up to the house in the morning, very early, while it was still dark, and hide it in the outhouse.

Granda

The back door flew open. Granda staggered in, his coat and cap covered in snow. He slammed the door behind him. Even in those few seconds, snow had blown into the kitchen and now began to melt.

Bonnie pulled out a chair for him to sit on, and knelt to help him take off his boots.

'Hands gone numb,' Granda said. He tucked them under his armpits to thaw them out.

'How many eggs today?' Bonnie asked. The hens laid fewer eggs now the daylight hours were so short.

Granda looked puzzled.

'I thought you were shutting the hens away,' Bonnie said.

Granda shook his head. His face was red with cold. 'I've been in the village hall. Border Guards' order. For the Registration.' He sounded tired out, Bonnie thought. And cross. Everything to do with the Border Guards made him cross. The way they ordered the village people around. Their stupid rules and punishments. The way they poked around and asked questions.

'I'll make you tea,' Bonnie said. She lifted the lid of the stove and peered in. The wood was glowing red-hot. She filled the kettle from the tap (their own spring water, sweet and fresh) and set it on the stove to heat up. She put a pinch of dried leaves into the blue pot.

Gradually, the kitchen warmed up. They sipped the hot tea without saying anything. Bonnie re-filled the pot.

'Where did you go today?' Granda spoke at last. 'We must be more careful, Bonnie. They've started counting people in and out.' His hands shook as he put the tea mug down on the table.

'What do you mean, counting?'

'The guards. They're keeping tabs on numbers. How many people live in the village. How many cross the border. Comings and goings. They're tightening the rules. And the school will notice if you miss too many days. They'll have to report it.'

Bonnie thought fast. 'Can't we say I'm ill? Or that I'm doing my learning at home, with you?'

'You learn more here than at that school, for sure. More that's useful and matters and makes you a happy person. But the guards won't understand any of that.' He sighed, a great weary sound.

'I'll make dinner, Granda, if you want to rest a bit more.'

'You're a good lass. So, where were you? I called and called, earlier. It was like you'd vanished into clean air.'

Bonnie laughed. 'Like the geese. Did you hear them? They flew right over the field and the house. They came with the snow.'

'Pink-foots? Good. Perhaps they'll stay around this winter. But we'll have to stop the shooters finding out.'

Shooters. She'd forgotten about the people who liked to kill the wild geese for sport. A pebble of fear lodged in Bonnie's chest.

'I went to the beach, earlier. I collected sea-leaves and crabs for soup. And I found some netting and two shoes.'

'Matching?'

'No. But leather. Good stuff.' She looked at Granda, saw suddenly how old and frail and weary he was. She hated to worry him more. She wouldn't mention the boat yet. But she did tell him about needing a new coat for the winter. 'I've outgrown everything, Granda. And it's much colder this year.'

Granda's eyes were red-ringed and watering. He needed glasses but they had long ago been broken and mended and broken again. It made everything such a struggle for him, not seeing properly. And maybe he wasn't hearing so well, either.

'Granda?'

But he had heard her. He spoke softly, as if the words hurt. 'Maybe now's the right time. You're old enough.' He cleared his throat. 'There's a box in the attic. Things Frances left behind. Clothes. See what fits. You're almost her size now. She'd want you to have her old things.'

Bonnie stared at Granda. 'Why didn't you tell me about it before?'

'I . . . I don't know, Bonnie. I was waiting for you to be older, I guess.' He shook his head. 'Go carefully up there.'

Bonnie thought about the box while she made the soup, and while they ate, and afterwards, while she washed the pots. It had been in the attic all these years and she hadn't known. What else might be there, as well as clothes? A letter from her mam? Books or photos?

She waited till Granda was settled in his chair by the fire with the lamp and his books, and then she climbed the stairs. She got out the ladder from the cupboard and set it under the attic hatch, like she'd seen Granda do. She lit the lamp from her bedroom and set that down at the foot of the ladder. It cast dancing shadows as she climbed up. She heaved the hatch door and pushed it back. A cold draught of air rushed out. She went back for the lamp and carefully put it inside the attic on the boards she could feel at the side of the opening. Not all the attic space was boarded: she knew she must tread very carefully so as not to plummet through the thin plaster of the ceiling below. She hauled herself up from the top of the ladder into the attic, and for one horrible moment she dangled there, in the space between, before she got the strength to pull herself right up inside.

It was cold and dark and cobwebby; she could see that much. The boards went round the edges of the attic, and as her eyes adjusted she saw bits of furniture—a baby's cot, and a chest of drawers, a chair covered in a dust sheet. And there in the corner was a rectangular wooden box. She moved the lamp closer. Dust motes spun in the small circle of light.

She opened the lid.

She lifted the sheet of polythene on top. Her hand brushed something soft and textured—a woollen jumper. She held it against her. Much too big, but soft and warm and thick. She laid it to one side. Three thin cotton dresses were next, and two skirts. Underneath those she found a coat—thick, made of a sheepskin, furry on the inside. She lifted it out and tried it. Too big, but so cosy. And so much warmer than her old coat. With difficulty, she folded back the sleeves. There. That was better. She kept it on as she delved deeper into the box. There was underwear, wrapped in tissue paper, and woollen socks, which would be wonderful—almost good as new! She'd never had anything new her whole life. Underneath that, she found a square flat cardboard box. She lifted the lid. Baby clothes. Little hats and mittens and jumpers, all made of wool, all so tiny they must have been made for a newborn baby, but they looked new, as if they'd never been worn. Bonnie put them back inside the box and closed the lid. It was like seeing something she wasn't meant to see. She rummaged underneath and at the very bottom she found a pair of ankle boots.

She pulled them on, and a shiver ran down her spine. Her feet were exactly where her mam's feet had been. For the very first time, her mam seemed like a real person, living and breathing, instead of someone from a story.

The boots were only slightly too big. The leather was soft, and the soles were thick and strong and hardly worn. She shifted her feet and walked a couple of steps. She went back to the box and ran her hand over the wooden bottom, searching for a letter or a photo or something more than clothes. But there was nothing.

'Bonnie?' Granda called.

She walked along the boards to the hatch, crouching under the slope of the roof. 'I'm in the attic looking at the clothes.'

Granda trudged slowly upstairs.

She waved as he came into view. 'There's a coat, and boots!'

He nodded. 'Be careful on the ladder, coming down.'

'Can you catch these?' Bonnie threw down the bundle of jumper and dresses, the underwear and socks, and Granda caught them and clasped them to him, as if he were hugging her mam.

Bonnie clambered down, closing the hatch as she went. She twirled round to show him the lovely coat and boots.

His voice choked as he admired them. 'For just a second, when you came down that ladder, I thought it was her all those years ago.'

'Do I look like her?' Bonnie asked later, when they were both sitting by the fire. 'Have you got other pictures of her, not just that little one by your bed?'

'Granda?'

There were tears on his cheeks. She took his hand and held it tight. 'I'm sorry,' she said. 'I didn't mean to make you sad.'

He squeezed her hand. 'It's such a long time since she left,' he said. 'I think of her every day. I hope she's safe and happy somewhere, but it's hard, not knowing. Never hearing anything.'

Bonnie nodded.

'We once had photos on laptops and phones but all that got lost.' He sighed. 'There might be some other photos from when she was a girl. I'll have a look tomorrow, in the daylight.' He rested his hand on her head lightly. 'You've her dark curly hair, Bonnie, and bright eyes, and the way you laugh and how you move so quick and light is just like her.' He smiled. 'Only, you are more patient. She was—impetuous. Angry at how things were changing. She was good at telling stories, mind you. Making things up. Imagining.'

'I do that too.'

'Yes. And that's exactly what they want to crush out of you.'

Bonnie thought about school; the tedious reciting of *The Rules of Civil Conduct* each morning, copying out long chunks of *The Duties of Citizenship*. Chanting the times tables. Handwriting drill. The long hours, sitting silent and still in rows. She shuddered.

'It's late,' Granda said. 'We should get some sleep. You go on up. I'll sort things down here. Night night, Bonnie love.'

On her way upstairs, Bonnie ran her hand over the soft sheepskin coat hanging on the stair post. She whispered the words *Night night, Mam*, as if trying them out for size.

The bedclothes were freezing. She lay under the clammy duvet and blankets and shivered in the dark. Outside, an owl hooted to another. Through the window she could see the snow still falling steadily. She imagined it piling up thick and soft and deep in the lane, on the fields, on the sand dunes. The geese would be cold and hungry. She thought of the little boat under its covering of snow, waiting for her.

Early

It was deeply quiet and cold, but the room was full of light. Was it morning already?

Bonnie knelt up to look out of the window, keeping the covers wrapped around her. Moonlight reflected off the snow: not sunrise, yet. And the quiet would be because of the deep snow, muffling the usual early morning sound of trucks along the main road.

The house was silent. Granda must be still asleep. She dressed quickly and ran down to the kitchen to get her boots. She put on the new coat and hugged its warmth to her. She scribbled a note—*Gone foraging at the beach. Will feed hens x*—and left it on the kitchen table.

The air outside was freezing. Her boots sank deep in the snow as she crossed the yard to the big shed. The hens greeted her with their gentle clucks. They clustered round her, crooning. 'Hello hens,' she said softly. 'Breakfast time!' She put a scoop of meal in their hopper, and checked the nest box for eggs, but there were none. The hens had been free to roam all night—usually Granda locked them in the henhouse overnight, in case a fox got in through the loose boards of the shed—and so the eggs, if there were any, might be hidden in the straw or under the old bits of machinery and tools or anywhere, but she didn't linger to look. She took a length of rope from a hook, coiled it loosely over her shoulder, and set off for the beach.

Each step, Bonnie loved the moment her boot crunched through the hard crust and then sank deep into softer snow. But it meant she was leaving tracks that anyone could see and follow. She checked behind her every few minutes, but no one seemed to be up yet. Moonlight cast shadows of blue. Other animals had passed this way: she could make out the tracks of a fox or a dog, and the light arrows made by bird feet. Bonnie went the same way she'd come back yesterday, dodging the village. Everything looked different, covered in deep snow. She found the track between the hawthorn trees to the field. She stopped to catch her breath.

The flock of geese had roosted at the edge of the field close to the dunes, where the wind had blown the snow and grass poked through. They shuffled their pink feet and called to each other as she got closer, but they did not fly off. Bonnie knew how to be calm and quiet around wild creatures. She watched them for a few minutes. How beautiful they were, with their pale blue-grey wings and dark heads. And then she hurried on, over the dune path, towards the boat.

The sky was lighter now, the setting moon a pale ghost of itself as the sun rose pink and gold and glorious above the sea, and turned the water into liquid colour. She stopped to watch it for a moment, then ran on.

A flutter of movement ahead made her stop again.

She crouched down, to wait and watch.

Was it a seal? It was something much bigger than a goose. But it had moved more quickly and deftly than a seal on land, and in any case, seals were rare and hardly ever seen. It was dark against the snow.

There! Again.

Something—someone—darted out from behind the snow-covered mound that must be her boat.

Bonnie was filled with fury. Someone had claimed the boat, when in truth it was her finding. But she didn't run or shout. She remembered everything that she had learned from Granda about waiting patiently, watching, gathering facts.

She edged closer to the dunes. What were they doing?

The person was smallish, thin—more her size than adult. Dark hair. Dark clothes. Darting about as if cold, or looking for something, oblivious to the fact they were being watched.

They shoved the boat, and jumped back as an avalanche of snow cascaded onto them.

For a second Bonnie wanted to laugh.

Everything was a blur of white.

She peered again. The person had gone.

Bonnie waited and watched, to be sure.

Nothing moved.

She crept closer, moving quietly from one clump of snowy dune grass to the next all along the top of the beach until she was close enough to make out human footprints. Bare feet, it looked like, not boots. In snow?

She sat very still, very quiet, for ages. Her feet and hands were numb with cold. More snow clouds were building on the horizon: the sky had turned yellow-grey.

The person had either run away, or they'd hidden under the upturned hull of the boat. She was almost certain it wasn't anyone she knew from the school or the village.

Perhaps they'd seen her, and were waiting for her to go.

She heard movement: a *thump*, and a soft whimper, like someone hurt or scared. And then a head appeared from the dark space under the boat.

She saw the mop of dark hair. Sunken cheeks. Dark eyes.

A thin boy, shaking with cold or fear, stared back at her. A stranger.

'It's OK,' she said softly, in the same tone she used for wild creatures, or hens. 'I won't hurt you.'

She thought of what happens when you corner a wild creature, and how an animal in pain will bite or kick, and so she stepped back. She smiled, to show him she meant no harm. She held out her empty hands: no stick or stone.

He was shivering. His feet were bare. His clothes were torn. She was sure he hadn't eaten for a long time. But he seemed intent on moving the boat. He pushed it and rocked it back and forth, loosening it from the snow and sand. He lifted it up from one end, and with a deft shove he flipped it right over. He must be much stronger than he looked. He began to push the boat away from the dunes, away from her, down the beach.

Bonnie saw at once what he meant to do; he'd get the boat into the sea, he'd float it away from the beach, and all the hopes and dreams she'd pinned on the boat would float away too.

'NO!' she shouted. 'It's MY boat. I found it. MINE.'

The boy stopped pushing the boat. He stared at her.

Bonnie rushed forward. She gripped the rim of the boat with both hands. She was fierce with anger. She was so close she could smell him—a mix of sweat and fish and wood smoke. She glared at him. 'LET GO OF MY BOAT!' she said, each word as clear and strong as she could make it.

'NO.' He spoke her language awkwardly. 'This is MY boat. I come in this boat.'

Bonnie wavered. Could that be true?

'Lost,' the boy said. 'Tired. But I go now, find different beach.'

Bonnie saw the tears in his eyes, the weariness, the resigned shrug of his shoulders.

She believed him. Of course it was his boat. He'd floated or rowed here and he was tired to the bone and he'd come ashore to rest. He must have been hiding underneath it yesterday, and huddled there all night, in the snow, alone in the dark.

But it was hard to know the boat wasn't hers, after all.

She stared at him.

He stared back.

She nodded. She let go of the side of the boat. She stepped back.

'Where have you come from?' she whispered. 'Where are you going?'

The boy didn't answer. He was studying the sky.

The first flakes of the snowstorm whirled over the sea, closing in like a white fog.

Bonnie knew it would be mad to try to row a boat out at sea when you can hardly see three boat lengths in front of you. There were rocks all along this coast. The boat would founder and the boy would drown and it would be her fault.

'Stay,' she said. 'I will help you.'

She winced as she glimpsed huge raw blisters on the palms of his hands. A gash on his ankle, swollen and bruised.

'Come back with me. I will find you a safe place to rest, and get you food.'

Had he understood? He kept looking at the sea, at the swirling snow, and back to her, studying her face as if searching the weather there, too.

'Trust me,' she said.

How could she show him she meant no harm?

She should give him something.

She put her hand in one of the deep pockets in the new coat, fished inside it even though she knew she had put nothing in there. And yet her fingers did find something, small and round and hard, deep in the seam of the pocket. She drew it out and looked at it.

A button. A conker-brown leather button. Her mam must have put it there, years ago.

What good was a button to a hungry frightened boy? She held it out to him anyway, as a token of trust.

He took it from her, and he put it in his own pocket.

'Come. We should go,' Bonnie said. 'Before someone sees us.'

'NO.' The boy shrank back from her. 'MY boat. Stay here, hide boat here.'

He didn't trust her after all.

'But it's not safe here. We can hide at my house.'

Did he understand? She tried again. 'It's too dangerous on the beach,' she said. 'People will take your boat away if they find it here. They might take you. You don't want that. It's forbidden to land at this beach.'

The boy listened intently.

'We can bring the boat with us,' Bonnie said. 'You and your boat, we'll hide you in a safe place. I can get you food.'

The boy nodded.

Bonnie smiled, to encourage him. 'We can drag it over the snow. That's what this rope is for.' She lifted the heavy coil over her head, and showed him what she meant. She tied the rope on the metal ring at the front of the boat, and tugged it.

The boy watched.

He undid her knot, and wound the rope a different way, so they could pull the boat together. He gave her one end of rope and kept the other himself. He showed her how to put it over one shoulder, so her whole body was taking the weight.

Between them, they dragged the boat up the beach towards the path. Bonnie stopped briefly to show him the Border Notice. She read the words aloud.

IT IS ILLEGAL TO LAND ON THIS BEACH WITHOUT A PERMIT. ALL INCOMERS MUST REPORT IMMEDIATELY TO THE BORDER GUARDS WITH CORRECT DOCUMENTATION. NO DOGS OR LIVESTOCK MAY BE BROUGHT ASHORE.

The boy shrugged. Maybe he hadn't understood.

They pressed on. It got easier once they reached the deeper snow. The boat slid like a big wooden sledge on runners, only much bulkier and heavier. Bonnie's arms and shoulders and back ached.

The boy stopped dead when he saw the first of the village houses. He let the rope slip from his hand. He turned towards the beach as if he wanted to run back there.

'It's OK,' Bonnie said. 'No one will be out yet. Too early and too cold.'

This boy had no papers; nothing more than his tattered clothes and his boat. If the Border Guards saw him, they'd take him away immediately. Confiscate the boat.

'Come on.' She tried to move the boat by herself, but it was too heavy and it slid sideways.

The boy seemed to decide something. He picked up his end of the rope and hauled it over his shoulder and started to pull with her again.

'Not far now,' Bonnie said.

The snow fell in soft flakes, straight down. There was no wind. If the snow kept falling like this it would cover their tracks.

At the garden gate, Bonnie stopped. 'Wait here. Don't move.'

She looked back when she reached the house. From here, the boy and the boat were simply dark shadows near the snowy hedge.

She opened the door and peered in. 'Granda?' she called, but there was no answer. She took a heavy iron key from the hook in the kitchen and went back out to get the boy.

She led the way, skirting the vegetable patch, now nothing but a snowy waste with a few wizened stumps of sprout stems poking through. The boat seemed heavier than ever. The boy was nervous, twitchy. She took him to the tumbledown outhouse at the very edge of their land, near a line of bare trees, and unlocked the wooden door. She checked behind them again, but there was no one around, no footprints but theirs, no sign of Granda.

Together they shoved and dragged the boat over the threshold into the outhouse. The boy had been silent for ages, but he made a scared sound, a kind of groan, when Bonnie closed the door behind them and shut out the light.

It was barely less cold than outside. Too many gaps in the wood, and draughts under the door, between broken planks, under ill-fitting roof slates. But it was dry at least, and out of the wind, and secret. No one would know a boat and a boy were hiding inside. No one would think to look. Granda never came here these days—there was no call to, since the outhouse was empty.

The boy climbed into the boat and sat hunched up, as if he felt safer there.

'I'll get you food,' she told him. 'And warm dry clothes. You must stay here. I have to lock the door, understand?'

The boy nodded.

It felt horrible, locking him in, but it was for his own safety, Bonnie told herself. Already she was planning what to take him: hot soup, the leftovers from last night, a mug of tea, bread. Her old coat, better than nothing, and she'd see if there were some old boots or shoes that Granda wouldn't miss. Thick socks. A blanket.

She ran back across the garden, scuffing the tracks the boat and their feet had made, so no one could possibly suspect anything. She stamped her snowy boots on the step, and pushed open the door.

Voices.

She listened, heart hammering.

No one ever visited, these days.

She heard Granda's voice, and someone else. Someone angry.

Granda started talking loudly, slowly, as if he were talking to someone stupid. 'She is my grandchild. And she is under my care.'

Should she run back out? Hide?

Too late.

The front room door opened. Bonnie froze.

Granda stood in the hall, staring at her, his eyes watery, trying to tell her something, but she could not understand what, and by then it was too late. A tall man with a thin pale face stepped out of the living room into the hall. The man had seen her too.

Eggs

'I've fed the hens, Granda,' Bonnie said. 'But there's still no eggs.' Her voice shook. She was lying.

'Thank you, Bonnie, but you should not have gone out in the cold, you being so unwell.' Granda was lying too. He was helping her out.

She played along. 'But you've got such a bad cough, Granda. And I went straight there and back.'

The man watched them. Did he guess it was all made up?

Bonnie had never seen him before. His thick grey coat was buttoned up to the neck, his trousers tucked into black boots. His nose twitched, as if he was trying to sniff out something.

'Take off your snowy things and go straight back to bed, Bonnie,' Granda said. 'I'll bring up some hot tea soon as we're done here. This is Mr Watts, from the School Authority Board. He's come about your absence from school.' He turned to face the man. 'Bonnie cannot come to school while she is infectious.'

Bonnie nodded. She tried to look like she might be.

The man frowned. 'Infectious?' He took a step back. 'What kind of infection?

'Fever. Temperature. Rash,' Granda said. 'We don't want to pass it on to the other children.'

The man backed away further, towards the door. 'This girl missed school yesterday. It is not acceptable. The school tests are imminent. Her teachers will set work to be done at home. You must collect it from the school today.'

'Not while she's ill,' Granda said. 'She must recover her strength properly first.'

'She must not fall further behind with her lessons,' the man snapped.

'Upstairs, now!' Granda told Bonnie.

She ran upstairs to her bedroom. Horrible man. She took off the sheepskin coat and her boots. She crept under the covers. Her hands and toes were numb with cold.

She worried about the boy, shivering in the outhouse, wondering where she'd gone. Scared, locked in. She heard the rise and fall of Granda's voice arguing with the man downstairs. At last, the front door slammed shut.

Granda shuffled slowly up the stairs. He stood in her bedroom doorway. His face was pale. He looked ill. He coughed for real. 'Oh Bonnie,' he said. 'We have to be very careful, now.'

'Why? What did he say?'

'Blathering nonsense, that's what. School attendance and discipline and tests. Hygiene procedures to deal with cases of infection. Even suggested I'm too old and feeble to look after you properly.'

Bonnie climbed out of bed. She hugged him. 'You're the best, most lovely granda in the world. And you do look after me.'

'We look after each other,' Granda said.

'What did you tell him about me being ill?'

Granda sighed. 'I said the first thing that came into my head. I said you were sick. I told him you were ill in bed. And then you walked in the back door. Oh Bonnie!' Granda laughed. 'But I think we fooled him. And he won't want to risk catching any infectious diseases from us. So we're safe for now.'

'Phew,' Bonnie said. 'And we can pretend I'm ill for weeks and weeks! I can stay hidden. I'm good at that.'

'Mebbe. So, where were you really, Bonnie, so early this snowy morning?'

'I wanted to walk in the deep snow! And it was really fun. I went to see if the geese were on the field, and they were. And I walked on the beach to look for treasure washed up, like always.'

'And did you find some?'

'I did. I found a button in the coat pocket, that my mam must have put there. And I found a boat and a boy from the sea and I brought them back here so we can help him and maybe use his boat for fishing and going on voyages.' She spoke in a big rush of words. Bonnie told him the truth, but in a way that made it sound like something she'd made up.

Granda smiled, as she knew he would, and he ruffled her hair. 'A likely tale! In this weather! You are a great one for telling stories!'

'So are you!' Bonnie hugged Granda. 'About my infectious illness and all.'

'Seeing as you're not going to school today, we can do other things, Bonnie.'

'Like what?'

'I'll look for some old pictures of your mam. And you can read and draw and write more stories.'

Bonnie waited till she heard Granda busy going through his boxes of old things. She gathered up clothes for the boy: her old coat, which she put on underneath her new sheepskin one, and the warm jumper and a pair of woollen socks from the box in the attic. She boiled the kettle to make tea, and cut a hunk of bread from yesterday's loaf. She found a small round goats' cheese, and picked out two wizened apples from the larder store. She bundled everything into the egg basket and soon as it was ready, poured the hot tea into an old jam jar with a screw lid. She pulled on her wet boots and laced them up and slipped out of the back door.

The snow whirled around her in a blizzard. She ran straight to the hen shed, checked no one was around, dodged behind it and made her way through the deep drifts to the line of trees and the far outhouse. She listened for a moment. Nothing. She unlocked the door.

The boy was exactly where she'd left him. For a

horrible second she wondered whether he'd died of cold. But he lifted his head. His eyes looked blank.

'I'm sorry, I came as quick as I could; it's complicated. Here's food and some tea.' She unpacked the basket, laid everything out on the seat in the boat. She took the socks from her pocket, and took off both coats and draped the smaller one with the hood over the edge of the boat, along with the jumper.

He stared at her. He didn't speak.

'Start with the tea,' Bonnie said. She lifted the jar for him and unscrewed the lid. 'It's still hot. It will warm your hands as well as your insides.'

He took it. He held it in both hands and winced with pain.

'Next time, I'll bring ointment for your hands and ankle,' she told him. 'And a blanket.'

She watched as he took small sips of tea, and then bigger gulps.

'How long since you ate anything?' she asked. 'You have to be careful if it's been a long time. Go slowly at first. Just a little bread, so you're not sick.'

But he was already cramming the cheese into his mouth, tearing the bread and shoving it in, and he took no notice of her.

'I can't stay,' she said. 'My granda's at home. He'll be looking for me. I'll come and see you later. Put the warm clothes on. Try to sleep.'

The boy kept eating.

'I've got to go, and you must stay very quiet. OK?'

The boy didn't answer.

'What's your name?' she said when she was at the door, ready to leave. 'I'm Bonnie.'

She should go, but she waited a little longer.

He swallowed a last mouthful of bread. 'Ish,' he said quietly.

She ran back to the hen shed. *Ish*. Was that a name? Or was he saying something else? Perhaps it meant *thanks*, or *come back soon*, or *goodbye* in another language.

She hated locking the door on him. The way he looked at her as she closed the door. Supposing he needed the loo. And she'd forgotten shoes for him, and a blanket. Later, she'd take those things, and more food and some water and ointment for his hands.

She unlocked the shed door. The hens clucked and chirruped around her. They'd been left out again. Granda had forgotten about them. Perhaps she should take over the hens at night as well as morning. One of the red hens was making a big fuss, tucked in the corner beneath the wheelbarrow. That meant one thing. Bonnie shooed her away, and picked up the still-warm egg, smooth and brown and beautiful in her hand. 'Thank you,' she told the hen. 'That can be for the boy.'

She hunted for more eggs. She found three hidden under a pile of straw, cold to touch. She put them in the basket. She filled the food hopper and broke the ice on the water dish and the hens crowded round to drink. She picked up her favourite hen, the one with black feathers that gleamed green in sunlight, and rested her cheek against its warm feathery body. 'Hello, Fritha,' she whispered. Granda said it was better not to give the hens names, because it made it even harder when it was time to cull them for meat. 'I won't let that happen to you,' she told the hen. She felt its quivering heart against her hand. Its eye was beady bright, edged with yellow. The hen listened to her voice and settled in her arms.

The hen shed seemed warmer than the outhouse where she'd left the boy. She supposed the hens' warm bodies made a difference, and the bales of straw. But he was safer there, and that was what mattered most.

Bonnie put the hen back down on the wooden floor

and watched it run to join the others at the food hopper. She sniffed. The shed needed a proper clean out.

Bonnie locked the door behind her and ran across the yard to the house.

'Four eggs this morning, Granda!' she called from the warm kitchen.

'Good. Come and see what I've found,' Granda called back.

The living room floor was scattered with photos and scraps of paper: old-fashioned letters.

'Here she is, about fifteen. Isn't she lovely?' Granda handed Bonnie one of the photos.

Bonnie peered at the serious face, the dark eyes and shoulder-length wavy dark hair, the long fringe. The girl wore a white shirt and a blue jumper. It was the oddest thing, looking at a teenage girl who was also her mam.

'Must be a school photo,' Granda said. He held out another.

'She looks more like me here,' Bonnie said. In this one, Mam was younger, maybe twelve or thirteen. Her hair was wild and wind-blown. She was smiling at the camera. She had one arm around a black-and-white sheepdog. Behind her was the sea.

'That's our beach!' Bonnie smiled. 'Was that her dog?'

Granda shook his head. 'That dog belonged to the lad up at the big house. Pilot, the dog was called. The family moved away and the house fell to ruin.' He coughed. 'That was before they closed the borders. People came and went wherever and whenever they liked, back then.'

The boy. He'd managed to travel.

Bonnie knelt on the floor, picked up more photos, old and creased and faded. The life before she existed. She found one of Granda, looking young and healthy and happy. He was leaning against a wall, a woman next to him. 'Is that Granma?'

'Yes, that's my bonny lass.'

Bonnie had never known her. She'd died before Bonnie was born. She had no real memory of her mam, either. But she did remember something from when she was very little: someone warm and soft holding her very close. Their light breath on her face, a hand smoothing her head. Perhaps that had been her mam.

'Here's a picture of the boat I've told you about,' Granda said.

The wooden rowing boat was a traditional coble, made of wood, flat-bottomed, which made it easier to launch from a beach into breaking seas, for fishing and trips to the islands.

'That boat meant *food*—fresh fish—and the freedom of the sea,' Granda said. 'And then your mam rowed away in it and disappeared forever.'

Bonnie waited. She was sure there was more. Perhaps this time Granda would tell her the whole story. 'And she left me behind.'

'She did. You were much too little to go on such a dangerous journey, and I would not let her risk your life, Bonnie, even if I could not stop her risking her own. You were too precious.'

'She wanted to take me, but you wouldn't let her.'

Granda sighed. 'We had a big fight about it. Maybe I was wrong. Maybe I should have let you go with your mam.' His voice trembled. 'I would have lost everything, Bonnie. And you are my pearl beyond price.'

'I was fast asleep, the night she left, so she could have taken you, but she didn't. She listened to me, and left her most precious thing in my safekeeping. You, her daughter.' Granda wiped his watery eyes. He stood up and stretched out his spine. 'That's enough for now, Bonnie. I'll go and make us a pot of tea.'

Bonnie leafed through the old letters and papers. Some

were still in their envelopes, with stamps and postmarks. In those days you could post a letter to someone and it would be delivered to their house the next day. She found a letter written to Granda by her mam when she was a girl. The handwriting was loopy and messy, not like the neat script Bonnie had to practise at school. Bonnie checked the postmark on the envelope but could not make out the name of the place. In the letter, her mam was on a trip somewhere, making fires for cooking outside and building shelters and kayaking on a river. She had a best friend called Olivia. She signed her name at the end—

Love you, Dad. See you soon, Frances xxx

Bonnie traced the words with her finger and whispered them into the room. *See you soon. Love.*

Granda came back with two mugs of tea. 'What you found there, Bonnie?'

'An old letter to you.'

'I kept them all. Silly really. What's the use?'

'It's nice,' Bonnie said. 'It's a little bit of her.'

'There's others,' Granda said. 'Letters from her friends, old boyfriends. I haven't touched those. They're her private things. But I keep 'em safe.'

'In case she comes back?'

'It's ten years or more, Bonnie. We'd have heard something. She's not coming back.'

Bonnie put the eggs into a pan on the stove in the kitchen and waited for the water to boil. There might be clues about Mam in those letters. Granda had said that she had no idea where she would go, beyond leaving this place and crossing the sea to a new land and a better life. She'd come back for Bonnie and Granda when she was settled. That was all she'd told him.

Bonnie found the big blue book of maps of the world on Granda's bookshelf, and turned the pages. So many pages. Mam could be anywhere. And the boy, where had he come from? She traced a straight line from their beach, out to sea, on the map of their land, and saw the other side of this sea, so very far away, the ice lands where the geese migrated from in winter. But maybe you could cross sea and land and go anywhere in the whole wide world, if you had the will, and the wit, and people to help, and a way to keep hidden from the Authorities who wanted everyone to stay where they were born and could be counted and controlled.

She took one of the hard-boiled eggs and tucked it

into her coat pocket. She ran upstairs to Granda's room and hunted in his cupboard for old shoes or boots, but there were none that he didn't need. Her own old shoes were too small for the boy. She couldn't bear to give him the new boots she'd found in the attic box. Instead, she took the un-matched pair she'd found washed up, now dried and crispy from salt, and put them in a bundle with a woollen blanket from her own cupboard. She stopped at the top of the stairs.

Granda came out of the living room and went into the kitchen. 'Lunch time, Bonnie,' he called up to her.

There was no way she could escape to the outhouse now. The boy would have to wait.

6

Boy

Bonnie escaped outside at last. The snow had stopped, and the sky was clearing. Stars glittered in the gaps between clouds. The air smelled of frost. These were the short days, the long nights of winter. Sometimes it seemed that spring would never come.

The boy was not in the boat.

In the dark it was hard to make out anything. The boat was there, but otherwise the outhouse was empty. How was it possible? She'd locked the door.

She piled the stuff she'd brought for the boy inside the boat, and then she felt her way along the wooden sides of the outhouse, searching for gaps big enough for a boy to escape through. There were plenty of small gaps. In the back corner she found a place where the boards were loosely nailed and might have been pulled apart and then pushed back, so no one would notice from the outside. The boy must have squeezed through. He was thin enough.

Now he was in real danger.

Nowhere was as safe as this place, tucked away from the village and from prying eyes and Border Guards. And she'd been so kind to him, too, bringing clothes and food.

Stupid boy.

At least she had the boat. That had been all she'd wanted in the first place, after all.

She left the food and the calendula ointment and blanket just in case he came back. She locked the door behind her and went to clean the hen shed and lock the hens up for the night.

She tried to forget about the boy.

It was pitch black by the time she went back across the yard to the house. The snow had a thin crust. Each boot print was edged with ice. The moon had not yet risen.

After supper, she took the big blue atlas with her

into the living room where Granda had lit a fire for the evening. It took precious fuel, but tonight was extra cold.

People without fire and shelter could die of the cold.

Bonnie pored over the atlas. She turned the pages slowly, studying each map, tracing the red lines of the borders between countries, and the blue lines on blue, which showed the depth of the oceans between land masses. She leafed back again to the page that showed the map of their own country, found the cluster of islands offshore. She wondered which way the boy had come in his boat. With the tides, most likely, blown on the wind. And the wind had been from the north that day, bringing the snow, and the geese. Or he could've rowed up the coast from the south, keeping close to the shore, travelling at night so no one would see him. She wished she had asked him more questions.

She imagined him now, lost and frozen in the snowy fields and woods, or worse, caught by the guards at the edge of the village or at one of the border posts. She and Granda would be in terrible trouble if he said she'd found him and helped him hide. A heavy fine: money they couldn't pay. They might put Granda in prison, and she'd be made to live in the village as a looked-after child.

The damp wood steamed on the fire. Granda read

his book of poems with its golden lettering on the green spine. Every so often he read a poem aloud to Bonnie. He liked the ancient ones best, written in an older version of their own language. The words looked strange on the page, but when you read them aloud they made more sense. It didn't matter if you couldn't understand everything. 'That's poetry for you,' Granda said. 'Listen to the music of the words, Bonnie.'

He cam also stille
There his moder was
As dew in Aprille
That falleth on the grass.

The poem was about a mother and a baby.

Upstairs in the attic was that box of baby clothes. Not her old ones, but new ones, for a new baby.

Granda nodded in his chair by the fire. Bonnie edged to the door, keeping an eye on him. He was asleep; he didn't see her creep out of the room, and put on her coat and boots. She took the lamp from the hook by the back door, and closed the door gently behind her.

The cold took her breath away.

The lamp threw moving shadows over the silent garden as she ran.

The moment she unlocked the door, she saw the bundle of blanket on the floor of the outhouse in the beam of lamplight.

The boy sat up, startled. He shuffled back, still wrapped in the blanket.

'It's alright. It's me, Bonnie.'

He was still half asleep. Bewildered.

'You weren't here—I was worried—where did you go? Are you alright? It isn't safe to go out. No one must see you.' A rush of words, too many. But it was such a relief, to find him there.

He stared, rocking slightly. 'No,' he said. 'No one saw.'

Bonnie calmed down. She rested the lamp on the floor. She sat on the edge of the boat and it rocked under her. 'Where were you? Where did you go?'

'Out. To see what kind of place is this.' His voice sounded dry and scratchy. Bonnie passed him the bottle of water, and he gulped down what was left.

'Border Guards. Guns.'

'You saw them?' Bonnie panicked. 'They saw you?'

'No. I hide.'

'It's too dangerous. You mustn't try to escape. You can't get through the border without papers.'

'Papers?'

'Permission to cross. A reason for the journey. Your identity information. Address.'

The boy went quiet.

'So don't go out again. No one must know you are here. OK? It's too dangerous for me and my granda if they find out about you.'

The boy wouldn't speak.

'Did you eat the egg? And put the ointment on your hands? It will soothe them and help them heal.'

He shook his head. Bonnie found the jar of ointment and unscrewed the lid. She put a little on her own hands and rubbed it in, to show him what she meant.

He sniffed the stuff, and smeared some on his hands.

'Your ankle, too,' Bonnie said.

The wound was red raw and open, and the boy sucked in his breath in pain.

'It looks bad,' Bonnie said. 'You can get poisoned blood if you don't clean a wound properly. I'll bring some boiled water.'

'Salt,' the boy said.

'OK.'

Once, when her tooth had hurt, Granda had made her swill salt water round her mouth and it had helped the tooth and gum to heal. Salt was a good idea.

He asked her for salt. It was such a small thing, when he clearly needed so much more. A warm bed, hot food, water to wash in, someone to take care of him, help to get home. Bonnie felt the responsibility for the boy like a sudden weight.

'Tell me who you are,' she said.

'Ish,' the boy said. 'I tell you before.'

He was too tired. Too cold. He could barely keep his eyes open.

'We should talk more in the morning,' Bonnie said. 'Go back to sleep now. Don't go out again.'

'Leave the lamp,' Ish said. 'Please.'

'I can't. Someone might see the light. And we need this one in the house. I'm sorry.'

Ish closed his eyes. He curled into a tight ball under the blanket, turned his back on her.

Bonnie locked the door behind her. It was to stop someone finding Ish and the boat, she reminded herself. It was simply to keep him safe.

And the boat hidden.

She needed that boat.

She felt bad about taking away the light, even so.

Bonnie heard Granda coughing as she came in the back door. She hung the lamp on the hook and took off her snowy boots and coat. She filled the kettle.

'Bonnie? That you?'

'Yes, Granda.'

'What you doing?'

'Making some tea.'

Bonnie padded through to the living room. The fire had died right down but the room was still warm. Granda's book had slipped off his lap onto the floor. She picked it up and put it on the chair arm.

'You're a good lass, Bonnie.'

'Your cough sounds bad, Granda. You should stay inside while it's so cold. I'll do the hens at night as well as morning from now on.'

He didn't argue with her. He sipped his tea, and soon he climbed the stairs to bed, his breath wheezing in his chest. It was Bonnie who checked the kitchen stove, and put the guard on the living room fire, and blew out the lamp on the landing.

Her room was freezing. There was ice on the inside of the windows: beautiful, intricate frost flowers blooming over the glass. Bonnie half undressed. She kept on her leggings and long-sleeved top and socks and burrowed under the duvet and blanket. The boy might actually die of cold in their outhouse. It wasn't right. She'd have to find a way to bring him into the house, and she'd have to get Granda on her side. Surely he would understand. It was like when they took in the injured swan, or fledglings fallen from the nest. One year they'd raised an abandoned young deer until it was strong enough to survive on its own.

But she knew it wasn't really the same. There were no penalties for caring for a deer, or a bird with a broken wing. No one could stop them caring for a migrating swan, not even the Border Guards.

A stranger boy was a very different thing.

Sickness

Each morning for the next five days, Bonnie took food and fresh water and a jar of hot tea to Ish, and the same again in the evening when she went to shut the hens away. She visited him during the day, too, when Granda was busy doing other things and would not notice her absence. The freezing weather and Granda's hacking cough meant he went out much less than usual. Bonnie had to stay close to home in case anyone saw her and reported her to the School Authority.

Each time she unlocked the outhouse door, she found Ish slumped on the floor, wrapped in the blanket. His eyes looked more sunken and blank. He hardly spoke.

She began to dread going to see him, fearful of what she might find.

'What is wrong? Are you sick? Hungry? Is it the cold?'

Ish would not answer. She could not tell if it was because he did not understand her questions, or did not know how to tell her what was the matter. Perhaps he didn't know.

Perhaps it was because of being locked up. Like the injured whooper swan and the abandoned deer. *Food and rest isn't enough to keep them well*, Granda had said. *They need their freedom: their wild life.* As soon as the swan's wing healed, they let her go. They opened the makeshift pen and she flew away. Bonnie had watched her get smaller and smaller until she was a white dot in the blue sky, and that was the last they saw of her. With the deer, they opened the outhouse door and it stepped nervously out into the garden, looked about, then darted towards the open gate and ran away to the woods above the house. For a few days it had come back early each morning for food, and that had made Bonnie happy. But Granda had made her stop feeding the deer. 'It's better that they don't become tame. They are wild things. They have their own family—the herd.'

Ish must be horribly lonely. Homesick. Missing his family.

This morning, she carried the big blue atlas under her coat, and opened it out on the floor next to Ish. She turned to the page that showed the coastline, the beach, the islands offshore, and the ocean beyond. 'This is us, here.' She pointed to the dot that was the village. 'And this is where you landed. Our beach.'

Ish peered at the map. He traced the coastline with his finger. For the first time, a spark of light came in his eyes. He took the book from her and turned the pages, back and forth.

Bonnie poured Ish some tea from the big jam jar into a smaller cup that was easier to hold with his sore hands. 'Show me where you came from.'

He flipped through the pages, to countries she had never heard of, places with names she couldn't pronounce.

'All these lands, and all this sea.' The boy's head bent low over the maps.

'No, show me where YOU came from.'

He didn't understand what she wanted. Perhaps he had never seen an atlas of the world before. He just kept turning the pages, looking at all the places.

'You. Ish,' she said more slowly. 'Where is your home? Where your family live.'

Ish closed the book with a thud. 'Nowhere,' he said. And then he wouldn't say any more. He sank back, exhausted.

He drank the rest of the tea, and silently he ate the two boiled eggs she'd brought him.

Bonnie picked up the atlas and pored again over the map of their bit of coastline, and the sea beyond. She traced her finger along the line of the border. Perhaps he was too scared to tell her. He might be running away from something, or someone. Or maybe he was like her mam, seeking a new life in a new place. Or maybe he'd simply got lost.

Ish tried to stand up. His legs were too weak. He clutched onto the edge of the boat, and collapsed back to the floor, and that was when Bonnie glimpsed the wound on his ankle, festering, oozing pus, and she realized what was wrong. The boy was really sick, the infection spreading through his blood, dangerous and deadly.

Untreated, he could die.

All day, she worried over what to do. She needed medicine for the boy.

At last, in the afternoon while it was still light, Granda

put his coat on. 'I'll go and see what they've got at the shop,' he said. 'We need flour and yeast for bread, and something to eke out the sea harvest. We've eaten the last of the sprouts. The ground's frozen too hard for digging up parsnips.'

'Wrap up warm,' Bonnie said. She passed him his scarf and cap and gloves from the stove rail.

Granda hesitated at the door. 'Should I mebbe call in at the school? Get the work you're supposed to do.'

'No,' Bonnie said. 'I'm too ill, remember?'

'But it might keep them off our backs a bit longer,' Granda said. 'We don't want them coming round here again to check on us.'

Bonnie sighed. 'All right. But I'll not do the work.'

He looked so old and weary, trudging across the snowy garden wrapped up in his big coat. He stopped twice to cough. She waited until he'd gone through the gate and onto the footpath to the village, and then went back to the kitchen and opened the larder door to search for medicine.

One shelf was full of bottled fruit: plums, gooseberries, apples, and blackberries. Below that was the shelf with big pots for flour and rice, a packet of sea salt, the wooden box of apples, and a basket of garlic and onions, harvested last July. Three jars of honey: a reminder of sweet summer days and sunshine. Jars of homemade redcurrant, gooseberry, and raspberry jam. On the top shelf were the ointments and salves and medicines Granda made from herbs and flowers, or traded with other people in the village.

In the old days, people used antibiotic pills to treat an infection. But antibiotics had stopped working, and were no longer available. They'd gone back to using the old remedies.

Bonnie dragged a kitchen chair into the larder and climbed on it so she could see better what was there.

Pots of calendula ointment, made from marigold flowers. A dusty jar of liquid—Bonnie lifted it out and read the label written in Granda's shaky handwriting—*Echinacea, for colds and flu*. There was a clear liquid in a bottle labelled *Witch Hazel*, and a dusty bundle of twigs that smelled spicy. There was *cough linctus, made from heather and honey*, and pots of dried herbs: *chamomile, lemon balm, meadowsweet, raspberry leaf, lavender, ginger root (ground)*. Bonnie reached in further and felt around the back of the shelf. She found small paper packages containing sterile cloth bandages. Army surplus, it said on the packaging. Her fingers touched something square and solid—a book. She edged the book closer and lifted it down.

The book was heavy. It had a green cover, with the title in black lettering: `Cole's Herbal: a guide to medicinal uses of plants and herbs.`

Excellent. Bonnie climbed off the chair, put the book on the table and opened its pages. A sweet musty smell wafted up. Some of the pages were stuck together, where someone had dropped water on them a long time ago. Bonnie leafed through, looking for what it said about wounds. Eating food full of vitamin C, it said, was important in helping the body fight infection. Garlic was good, and fresh fruit and leafy green vegetables. Honey was a traditional aid to healing, especially a special kind of honey called Mānuka. Well, they didn't have that, but they did have honey from the hives at Long Barn. Echinacea, an infusion made from flowers, could help the body's own immune system to combat an infection.

Bonnie climbed back onto the chair, found the Echinacea bottle and carried it to the table. She unscrewed the top and sniffed. The liquid smelled like grass or wet leaves. You put drops of it into a cup of water, the book said, and drank it several times a day.

She looked up the uses of each of the dried herbs

on the shelf. Lavender made you calm and relaxed. Sage helped sore throats. Lots of the herbs were used in midwifery—for women having babies. Maybe Mam had taken them when Bonnie was born. The herbs looked dry and dusty. Most likely they wouldn't work after such a long time.

She packed the things she needed into a canvas bag: a jar of honey, bandages, the Echinacea. She boiled a kettle of water, poured it into a jar and added salt. She found some old cotton cloths in the drawer of the living room cupboard. She put her precious tin of coloured pencils and a roll of paper in the bag, too. She washed her hands properly, with soap and water, and put on her gloves.

It was beginning to get dark. She waded through the snow to the outhouse. She unlocked the door with shaky hands.

Ish was lying in the same position as she'd left him, the atlas open on the floor beside him. He didn't move.

'Ish?' Bonnie whispered. 'I've brought medicine and things to help you.'

He stirred, and Bonnie went closer. She crouched down next to him. 'We must wash your ankle with the salt water, and I'll wrap it in a bandage with honey on it, and then the wound will start to heal.' She unpacked the bag, showed him the medicine. 'I'll make soup with garlic tonight.'

Ish picked up the tin of pencils and opened the lid.

Bonnie unrolled the paper for him. 'When you're feeling better, you can draw and write. It will help make the time go quicker. You could write a note, even, to let your family know you're safe. They will be worried about you. And we can find someone to take it . . .'

Of course it would be impossible. But he'd have to write down an address. Assuming he could write. And that would tell her where he was from.

'When better, I will go,' Ish said. 'You will help me.'

Bonnie nodded. 'If I can.'

'Put your leg out straight,' she said. 'And grit your teeth. This is going to hurt.'

She unscrewed the jar of salt water, took off her gloves, and began to clean up the wound. It smelled foul. She had to turn her head away, and take deep breaths, and she had to ignore the tears running down Ish's face, as she cleaned the wound until the blood ran bright red and all the pus was wiped away.

She spread a layer of honey over the wound, and wrapped a bandage round, tight but not too tight, and then at last she could breathe freely. 'Much better now,' she told him.

She helped him get more comfortable. He sat against the boat with both legs stretched out. She propped up the damaged one so it rested on the atlas. She tucked the blanket around him.

'Now drink this.' She dripped ten drops of Echinacea into the cup of water.

She set a stub of candle on the floor, and showed him how to use the flint striker to make a spark. 'Only in an emergency,' she said. 'No one must see. But if the dark is unbearable, you can light it in the night.'

She placed the bottle of medicine and the pot of honey and spare bandages and cloths neatly in the bottom of the boat.

Ish closed his eyes. He seemed half asleep again already.

Bonnie bundled the dirty cloths into the bag.

'I won't lock the door. The guards haven't been walking this way since the snow. They're likely staying close to their posts.'

Ish opened his eyes briefly.

'Granda will be home any minute. I have to go. I'll try to come back with soup at dinner time.'

She closed the outhouse door quietly behind her, checked the garden was empty, and ran back to the house. She put the filthy smelly cloths into the kitchen stove and watched them burn. She washed her hands over and over, but it seemed the stench still clung to her skin, as if it was right inside her.

Fritha

Granda dumped his rucksack on the table. He lowered himself onto a chair. Bonnie helped him out of his coat and unlaced his boots.

Granda sighed. 'Well. Everyone in the school has heard about your illness, Bonnie. Your *fictitious* illness, I mean.'

'That's good, isn't it? They'll leave us alone.'

'Mebbe, mebbe not. They are afraid my cough means illness too. They wouldn't let me inside the school building. The assistant teacher eventually brought a stack of papers out to me, but I had to wait outside in the cold. They are monsters.' He fished the papers out of the bag and pushed them across the table to Bonnie.

'You're to do all the practice tests, and learn the spellings, and write a factual report on one of the topics on the list, using paragraphs and the three-part structure. Whatever that is.'

'I've no idea,' Bonnie said. 'And I'm not doing any of it. What's the point? I'll make soup instead.'

'You do that, pet.' Granda leant forward and took both Bonnie's hands in his. 'You're a good lass.'

'Your hands are freezing!'

Bonnie emptied the new paper sack of flour into the tin in the larder, and put the slab of yeast on a saucer on the shelf. She put a handful of carrots and a small butternut squash and a small bag of green lentils on the draining board.

'We're lucky to get those,' Granda told her. 'Someone I used to know from way back, from one of the inland farms, brought them to sell at the shop while I was there. It'll be a treat to have something tasty.'

Bonnie peeled and diced the squash and the carrots and put them in the stove pot with water and dried sage. She added three cloves of garlic, crushed with salt. 'That'll be good for your cough, Granda,' she told him. 'I've been reading about it. I found your old Herbal book.'

'Not mine,' Granda said. 'Your mam's.'

Bonnie stirred the soup. The liquid was a deep golden colour and smelled glorious. It would be good for Ish as well as Granda. Soup for healing.

'You're spending a lot of time with those hens, Bonnie,' Granda said, when she came back from the outhouse after dinner.

'I like it there. I like looking after things.'

'We should consider culling some for the pot. We've not had any meat or fish for days. You need the vitamins in the winter, especially when it's this cold. Chicken stew, and broth from the bones.'

'Not my Fritha,' Bonnie said. 'We're never going to eat her.'

'You shouldn't give the hens names, Bonnie. I told you before.'

Bonnie pouted. 'Well I did and that's that. Just one. Fritha.'

'Why did you call her that?'

'I liked the name. I read it in a book.'

'It was a name your mam liked too. But you couldn't have known that. It's an Old Norse name: means *beautiful*.'

'She is beautiful, my glossy black hen. Well, she will be, when spring comes again. The hens hate the snow and the cold. They're fed up with being in the shed.'

'I don't blame them,' Granda said. 'We'll all go cabin crazy if this snow doesn't let up soon.' He coughed and coughed.

Bonnie ran to fetch him a glass of water. 'Your cough's getting worse. You shouldn't go out in the cold, Granda.' She held the glass for him to sip. 'Don't try to talk.'

Granda slumped back in his chair.

Bonnie read poems aloud to him from his favourite book. She brought a blanket down from his bedroom and tucked it round his legs to make him cosy.

Granda seemed miles away, lost in thought, or perhaps he was dozing.

Bonnie put more logs on the fire and stirred the ash with the poker.

Granda shifted in the chair. He reached out for Bonnie's hand. 'The new baby would have been called Fritha,' he said.

'What new baby?'

'Your mam's.'

'Mam had a baby? I had a *sister*? Granda!'

'She only lived one week. It happened to so many

babes around that time. *The seven-day death*, people called it. We didn't know how to stop it, without antibiotics.'

Bonnie tried to make sense of what he was telling her. *A sister.*

'And that's the real reason Frances went, mebbe.'

'How old was I?' Bonnie asked.

'Two and a bit years. Little more than a babe yourself,' Granda said.

Bonnie tried to imagine herself, a two-year-old, with a mother and a brand new baby sister who was sick and died. She could not do it. There had only ever been her and Granda.

'Why didn't you tell me this before, Granda?'

'What good does it do? It complicates things. It's a grown up's story. The sadness doesn't belong to you, Bonnie.'

But she could not really feel sad about a sister she did not remember.

Her head reeled. 'Who was the baby's da? What happened to him?'

'Aidan. The lad from the big house. He went too, a year after the baby died; sailed away in his own boat to a new, better life. I used to wonder whether your mam went to join him, mebbe.'

Granda closed his eyes. He wouldn't say any more.

The shock of it!

In bed, Bonnie went over and over it all in her head. A sister who had lived only seven days, called Fritha.

Fritha. Those baby clothes in the attic, unworn, must have been meant for her.

And Fritha had a father.

She already knew about her own real father who had drowned before she was born. *The sea gives and the sea takes.* But now there was someone else—a man called Aidan, who had loved her mam. And if he was Fritha's father, that meant he was connected to Bonnie, too.

Part of her family.

If Granda had not seemed so old and frail tonight, she would have been angry with him for not telling her all this before. But then, she'd never really asked.

That moment she found the boat on the beach, everything changed forever.

The boat had called to her.

It had woken her up.

It had made her yearn for change and adventure, a bigger world.

The boy was part of all this too.

The wind rattled the glass panes in her icy bedroom. A vixen called from the snowy garden. Bonnie imagined it prowling around the hen shed, finding gaps between the wooden boards to squeeze through. Thank goodness she had locked the hens inside their house for the night. They'd be terrified by the fox, but they'd be safe.

And the boy would be huddled under the blanket in the cold and dark, planning his escape. The door was unlocked, but he was much too weak and ill to travel anywhere tonight. And there was no way he'd be able to move the boat by himself.

What if the medicine didn't work? What if he got sicker and sicker and died?

Bonnie could not sleep. She put on the sheepskin coat from the attic box, and two pairs of socks, and she padded downstairs into the living room. There was just a little warmth left in the fire. She lit a candle, and opened the drawer where Granda had put Mam's old letters. She lifted them out and started to read.

Letters

Letter after letter—she read them all. The candle burnt so low she had to light a new one. She stirred the embers of the fire and added another log. She heard Granda's wheezing cough from his room upstairs, and the creaking bedsprings as he turned over, and she listened carefully for sounds of him getting up, but he didn't.

Most of the letters were short, from Mam's friend Olivia, notes about school, and work, and plans for a party and other arrangements. Bonnie wondered what Olivia was like. She'd never had a best friend. She tried to imagine what it would be like to be so close to someone the same age as you; to tell them everything and to do things together.

There were the letters to Granda that Mam must have sent when she was on school trips. That was what schools did back then—went on journeys to different places, let children play and explore and learn things in different ways, outside.

And there was a small bundle of letters held together by a rubber band, written to *Frances* by someone who signed himself '*A*'.

Aidan?

These must be the letters Granda had never read.

Bonnie tried to ease the letters out of the band. The rubber was ancient: it snapped and the letters spilled out onto Bonnie's lap and over the floor. They were handwritten on pale blue paper, by someone not very good at writing. The words were scribbled all over the place, not in straight lines. Bonnie peered in the dim candlelight, trying to decipher the words.

There were tiny meticulous line drawings too, down the margins and sometimes as part of a sentence instead of a word. In black ink, small sketches of a dog, and a sea swallow, a deer with a fawn, a shell, a landscape with trees and a lake, a statue of a man and a lady in old-fashioned clothes holding each other very close. He said he was missing her. He thought of her all the time.

He would try to meet her after work. Things he had seen that day at work. Promises.

Love letters.

Now Bonnie understood what Granda had meant. It was like eavesdropping on someone's private conversation. It didn't feel right.

She scanned each letter quickly, in case there was more important information, or something about her. Or about a baby. But the person—*A*—didn't mention her name in any of the letters. There was nothing about a baby called Fritha, either.

Finally, she found one written on thin blue paper. She unfolded the single page.

I've made the log house warm and secure. Painted the doors and window frames blue. It's at the edge of a lake, with larch forest behind, and the small vegetable patch is already producing green salad shoots. We have fresh meat, too—deer and rabbits are plentiful and need to be kept in check, and there are wild ducks on the lake. There is space enough for you and a little one. Come before you're too far on to travel. It will be a new start. It is risky, *yes, but this is your chance to begin again. The journey by boat took less than a week with a fair wind. Spring is the best time. Don't leave it too late. A.*

Bonnie sat on the floor with the letter in her hand. The fire quietly turned to ash. The candle went out.

The chill in the room finally roused her. She bundled the letters back into the drawer. All except the last one. She folded the page again, and she shoved it deep into the pocket of the sheepskin coat.

She went over and over it in her head.

You and a little one. That must mean her, Bonnie. She was little, then. Two years old. So Aidan had wanted Mam to bring Bonnie with her.

And there was one sentence that didn't make any sense.

Come before you're too far on to travel.

What did that mean? *Too far on.*

Guards

BANG! BANG! BANG!

Bonnie woke with a start. Someone was hammering on the front door.

She ran to Granda's bedroom at the front of the house and pulled back the curtain just enough to peer down.

Two men in green uniform stood on the front step.

Bonnie ducked down.

'What is it?' Granda wheezed from the bed. 'Who's making that racket?'

'Border Guards,' Bonnie said. 'Two of them.'

'Blasted nuisance. I'd better see what they want.' Granda climbed out of bed. He wrapped a blanket round his shoulders and trudged slowly downstairs.

Bonnie hovered in the bedroom doorway, her heart thudding as she listened.

The guards talked in clipped voices. 'The inhabitants in this house are two persons.'

'Yes. Myself and my granddaughter.'

'Name? Age?'

'You know all this,' Granda said. 'I told you last week at the Registration.'

Don't make them angry! Bonnie willed him. *Just tell them what they want. Then they'll go away.*

'Names and ages.'

Granda coughed and coughed.

Bonnie ran down the stairs. Granda was doubled over with his cough. The men looked on without compassion.

'Matthew John Penn, 74. Bonnie Frances Penn, 13,' she gabbled.

The younger guard gave a curt nod. He ticked his list.

Bonnie patted Granda's back. 'Sit down, Granda. I'll get you some water.'

'That's it? No one else?' The guard stared at Bonnie.

Bonnie shook her head.

'A light was seen in this property late last night.'

Granda sighed. 'I read books, by candlelight. That's not a crime. Not yet.'

'Don't,' Bonnie whispered. 'Stay calm, Granda. You'll make yourself cough again.'

The guard shifted his feet slightly. 'There have been reports of unidentified persons in the border area. You are advised to keep doors locked. Sheds, outhouses, anywhere where strangers might try to hide. Report any suspicious sightings immediately.'

'Yes yes yes,' Granda muttered.

'For your own safety,' the guard snapped.

'Yes. We understand. Thank you,' Bonnie said. 'My granda isn't well. Is that all?'

The guard checked his list. He peered at her. 'Bonnie Penn. You have missed eight days' school attendance.'

How did he know that?

'You must obtain an official medical certificate for ill health, or return to school immediately.'

Bonnie nodded. The blood rushed to her cheeks. She wanted to slam the door in their horrible faces.

'Failure to do so will incur penalties for you, Mr Penn. You are responsible for her attendance, as the named adult guardian.'

'He's not well,' Bonnie said. 'And I have an infection. We can't go out to get a certificate till we're both better. We're contagious.'

The guard frowned. He took a step back.

The older one was already walking away.

Granda closed the front door so swiftly he clipped the tip of the young guard's boot. He turned back to Bonnie. 'You get dressed. I'll put on water for tea.'

'Now they'll be angry,' she said. 'They'll be prowling round again. Oh Granda! You have to be civil to the guards.'

'*I'm* angry!' Granda said. 'Officious idiots. Who do they think they are, speaking to us like that!' He carried on muttering as he walked into the kitchen.

Bonnie ran back upstairs to get dressed.

There were no new eggs to collect that morning. Perhaps last night's fox had put the hens off laying. Bonnie let them out into the barn to scratch around in the straw. She shovelled some of the dirty straw out onto the snow.

She and Granda ate slices of bread and honey for breakfast.

'We've hardly any fresh food left. I'll go down to the beach to see what I can find,' Bonnie said.

She made a honey sandwich for Ish and put it in her coat pocket.

Granda raised his eyebrows.

'A snack for later,' she said. She picked up the metal bucket for collecting the sea harvest.

Granda didn't say anything.

Bonnie checked he wasn't watching, crossed the yard to the hen shed, and waded round the back through the deep snow to the outhouse. She opened the door.

Ish was curled on the floor asleep. She put the honey sandwich on the edge of the boat for him to find when he woke up.

His face looked troubled, even in sleep. Maybe he was in pain.

On the floor next to him lay the open tin of coloured pencils and the roll of paper. Bonnie crept closer.

He'd done a whole series of drawings, like a cartoon strip. Frame after frame, in black and brown and red and orange pencil. A sky full of aeroplanes dropping bombs. Broken buildings. Fire. People running. The people were stick people, but with faces, open mouths, as if they were screaming. She couldn't see it all; the paper was still curled up from where it had been rolled.

Bonnie drew back.

Ish slept on.

She tiptoed away again. She closed the door behind her.

Her legs were shaking.

Bonnie tried not to think what the pictures meant. She made her mind go white and smooth and empty, like the snow.

It was days since she'd been down to the beach. And all those days, the snow had kept falling. Bonnie waded through the deep drifts blocking the footpath. The wind had whipped and shaped the snow into tall peaks against the hedge. She ploughed on down the path behind the village and on towards the beach. From the village came the sound of shovels scraping snow off tarmac, voices, the rattle of a truck engine left running.

Bonnie pulled up her hood and scurried on. No one must see her. She'd be too conspicuous this time of day, when all the other children would be in school. At least no one had come along the beach path: there were no footprints. It was so deep it was almost like swimming, plunging into drifts up to her waist.

Urgh! Her feet squelched in the melted snow inside her boots.

How odd it was to see the beach completely white, and the sea foam breaking onto snow. She waded along the shallows, searching for edible weed. She climbed onto the slippery rocks of the Whin Sill, peered into the rock pools, prised limpets off wet rock. *Sorry, Thank you.* Little by little, the sea delivered its harvest: enough to flavour a broth and add a little protein.

If only she had Ish's boat with her this morning. The sea was unusually calm: she could have launched the boat, cast a fishing line, even rowed all the way out to the islands where there would be all sorts of shellfish and crabs. She might have discovered fresh vegetables still growing in the sheltered walled garden left behind by the keeper who once lived in the house of light.

Bonnie stood at the sea edge, gazing out towards the wide ocean beyond. Maybe her mam was actually living the other side of that ocean. Maybe she walked down to the sea sometimes and thought of the daughter she'd had to leave behind. Maybe she was planning even now to come back to find her.

Far out at sea, she could just make out the ghostly shape of a huge tanker moving slowly northwards. Life was still going on out there: goods traded between countries, people moving from one place to another. There were still places in the world where people could be properly free, Granda said. Where there was fairness and justice, and people were valued; places where stories and literature and music and art were considered important.

Her mind turned again to the pictures Ish had drawn—the sketchy lines scribbled over the white paper. Images of war and terror. Destruction and death.

The sudden crack of gunshot echoed out over the sand.

Bonnie whipped round.

Geese whirred in the sky above the fields behind the dunes.

Shooters?

She was too exposed, out here alone on the beach. She scurried back up to the shelter of the dunes and crouched down, heart thudding.

She craned her head to listen.

She heard the faint drip of melting snow as it slid off the dune grass.

The sea shooshed onto the shore.

Nothing else.

She pictured in her mind the men who kill wild geese for sport. She imagined the hard metal bullets piercing the soft feathers and flesh of the defenceless birds. Those men seemed to enjoy the killing. It wasn't about food for them; they were rich people from big houses inland, with their own vehicles and guns and no shortage of meat.

She shuddered.

She crouched there a long time, shivering, listening.

The geese did not come back. They'd flown further inland. Maybe they'd rest on the lake, where they felt safer.

Her own heart settled to a steady rhythm.

Perhaps it had not been gunshot after all.

Even so, it had unnerved her. Anyone could be watching. Following her movements. She crept back through the dunes, plunging into deep snowdrifts and once falling over completely. She had to pick up everything that had dropped from the bucket: seaweed and shellfish and one tiny green crab. Gradually she found her way back to the path that ran behind the village and up to her and Granda's house on the edge.

There were voices coming from the village—excited voices, as if some sort of drama was going on and everyone was out on the streets to gossip about it. Shouts, like military orders, and then the rev of engines, and heavy tyres grinding along the road that went up the hill and along the border wall. Trucks, it sounded like, a whole series of them.

Bonnie checked no one was on the footpath ahead. She pulled her hood up and hurried on.

She was almost home.

She stopped.

There was blood in the snow: scarlet drops of fresh blood.

She stared at it.

She reasoned with herself: it might not mean anything. Maybe someone from the village had taken a shot at the fox who'd been prowling around.

She looked more closely. A spatter of blood, and then a trail of drips going up the path towards the woods, and marks in the snow like boot tracks—bigger than her feet.

Blood in the snow.

Her heart pounded.

Oh no. Not Ish. Please not.

One set of boot tracks went along the hedge and towards the woods, and another went into the garden.

The back door to the house opened.

'Bonnie!' Granda staggered across the garden towards her, calling her name, coughing and spluttering.

'Bonnie! Thank heaven! You were gone so long I came

out to look for you over an hour ago and found . . . all this!' He pointed to the blood. He hugged her tight.

Bonnie felt his ribs heave with each breath, heard the wheezing in his chest.

'My Bonnie,' he whispered. 'You're sure you're all right?'

'I'm fine, Granda. Let's go back inside.'

She took his hands and steered him back towards the house. 'You've got yourself all worked up. You're freezing cold. You shouldn't come outside with no coat or gloves. Whatever were you thinking!'

'There's all kinds of commotion going on in the village.' Granda's voice shook with another spasm of coughing. 'Something's up.'

Bonnie bundled him into the kitchen and onto a chair. She put another log on the stove. She filled the kettle. 'Sit there, Granda. I'll make us tea. I'm OK. It's all OK. The geese are still on the field. I heard something like gunshot and I thought it was shooters who'd found the geese but it wasn't. They've flown inland. We could go and watch them at that lake, maybe. The sea was really calm. I found some limpets and weed for the soup. There are massive snowdrifts in the lane like snow sculptures.'

She talked fast, all the time she was making tea, to

stop herself thinking about what might have happened to Ish. To stop the chatter in her head. *So stupid, to have left the door unlocked.*

A loud knock on the door made Granda spill his tea. 'Stay there,' Bonnie said. 'I'll go.'

Hiding Places

Bonnie eased open the door just a crack. A uniformed Border Guard was waiting on the step. Not one of the guards who'd come before; this one wasn't much more than a boy, with cropped hair and pale eyes.

'I'm ill,' Bonnie told him through the gap. 'Infectious.'

He nodded. 'Bonnie Frances Penn.'

'Yes.'

'I need to speak to your guardian.'

'Guardian? Oh, you mean Granda. He's ill too.'

The young guard seemed unsure what to do next.

Bonnie opened the door a bit wider. The guard stepped back, nervous. He spoke fast. 'There's a man on the run. Stay inside. He may be armed and dangerous.

Guards will be checking all houses, sheds, and outlying buildings.'

Bonnie nodded.

The young man gave a kind of salute as he left, as if he were a soldier. Or playing at soldiers, like the boys at school.

She shut the door fast. Her knees were trembling.

'What's going on?' Granda called from the kitchen.

Bonnie joined him at the kitchen table. She repeated what the guard had said.

'So they shot at some poor blighter, and he got away, is the sum of it,' Granda said. 'Well, good luck to him. Hope he does get away. Would hide him here in our attic if I could.'

'But they're checking all the houses.'

'Yes.'

'And the sheds.'

Granda looked at Bonnie. 'You may want to go and see to the hens, I guess. Make sure they're all comfortable and safe. Perhaps lock them in the henhouse, so they don't get spooked by any search parties.'

Bonnie nodded.

'Take your tea and a sandwich with you, eh?'

Bonnie nodded again.

He must have guessed. Somehow he knew about the boy in the outhouse.

'Hurry up, then,' Granda said. 'They'll be here poking their noses into our business any minute. Take the outhouse key. Keep everything locked. It buys us a little extra time.'

What did she expect? That Ish would be collapsed on the floor in a pool of blood? Or that he would not be there at all . . .

He was sitting on the floor against the boat, with his sore leg stretched out, and he was drawing with the blue pencil. 'Feel bit better today.' He smiled.

'Ish,' Bonnie said. 'We have to hide you. You can't stay here. The guards are searching all the sheds and houses. We have to be quick.'

He dropped the blue pencil.

'Hide where?'

'The attic,' Bonnie said.

Ish looked baffled.

'Attic. The loft. At the top of the house.'

He held onto the boat and pulled himself up. 'No. I stay with boat.'

'There's no choice. We have to save you. We can't take the boat. Now, come.'

Bonnie trembled with fear. The precious boat would be confiscated, and examined, and she and Granda would be taken away for questioning and the boy would be discovered and that would be it. The end.

Ish was already piling his few things into the boat— the blanket, the water bottle, the medicines, the stub of candle. He stuffed the flint striker into his pocket. He rolled up the paper and closed the lid on the pencil tin.

'I know hiding place,' he said. 'You and me, we push boat there. Over snow will be quick enough, yes.'

'What place?' Panic made her throat tighten. 'The guards will be here any minute.'

'Old big ruin house, no one lives there, up through trees.' Ish shoved the boat towards the door, slid it over the threshold and out onto the snow. He limped, as if every step hurt.

'You're still too sick . . .' she said. 'It's much too far. We'll never get there. This is too dangerous, Ish. It's crazy even to try!' But she heaved the boat along with him.

Ish wasn't strong enough on his own. She could hardly abandon him now. He deserved a chance. And if they could save the boat, well . . .

She locked the outhouse door behind them, put the key in her pocket, shoved and slid the boat across the garden. She glanced back twice to check the house. Snow was falling again, huge feathery flakes. The next time she looked, she thought she glimpsed Granda at the window, but she could not be sure. The fast-falling snow made everything blurred. There was no time to tell him what she was doing. Perhaps it was better if he didn't know.

The fresh snow had already hidden the spots of blood on the path. It would cover up the tracks of the boat, and Ish and her boot prints, too. Ish's ill-fitting shoes flapped and slid. She wished she'd found him something more weatherproof and warm.

They pushed and pulled the boat uphill. Bonnie pulled with the rope at the front, and Ish pushed the stern of the boat. The path got narrower. The snow was deep and the top was still frozen in places, and so the boat glided over the crust, then ploughed into massive drifts. They stopped frequently so Ish could rest his sore leg. He didn't complain but he winced with pain.

Instead of hedgerow either side of the path, now there were taller trees: ash and beech, alder and sycamore. Bonnie's heart hammered. She listened out for gunshot, or voices, or tramping feet.

Ish said nothing. He was getting weaker.

They got to the proper dense woodland, and she relaxed a bit. The trees were evergreen here: pine and fir planted close together a long time ago as a plantation, for logging. There seemed to be less snow under the deep shelter of the firs.

It was harder to push the boat, but it felt safer.

'Stop for a proper rest,' Bonnie said, once they were deep into the wood.

They sat on the edge of the boat. Ish stretched out his sore leg. The bandage was muddy and stained and soaked through.

'We'll put on a fresh bandage when we get there,' Bonnie said.

Ish nodded.

'How come you know about the house?'

'That night, first time I go out,' Ish said. 'I explore other places to hide. Walk long way through trees.'

'Granda took me there once.' She shivered. 'It was dark and damp and spooky. The roof had collapsed.'

'We make a roof,' Ish said. 'Is very hidden place, quite safe I think. No guards come there. Is safe from eyes and guns.'

'But I don't remember the way through the woods to

get there. I was only little. The trees are much bigger now and it's all wild and overgrown.'

They set off again.

The footpath petered out. There were animal tracks, but no clear way forward. They dragged the boat between tree trunks, zigzagging a way through the woods. They tripped over fallen branches hidden under snow. The boat snagged on the low branches of the trees. It suddenly seemed ridiculous to Bonnie, to be pushing a wooden boat into a wood, as if they were returning it to its own beginnings.

'I've no idea which way to go,' she finally said. 'I'm totally lost. It could be anywhere. The woods go on for miles, right up to the moorlands and the lake. But this doesn't feel right. They're the wrong kind of trees. The house is in other kinds of woods, oak and ash and holly, not evergreen fir.'

Ish was lost too. He looked exhausted. Defeated.

Bonnie fished in her pocket. 'Here, she said. 'I forgot, sorry. This was for you.'

Ish took the squashed honey sandwich and divided it in two. 'We share,' he said. He insisted.

The honey tasted sweet and delicious.

'You wait here with the boat,' Bonnie said, 'while

I try to find which way to go. I'll come back to get you.'

She looked back once. Ish was lying in the boat. Good. He badly needed the rest. It was amazing he'd made it this far.

Even from these few yards away, the boat seemed to blend in among the firs, camouflaged against the rough tree trunks.

Bonnie remembered the old stories about getting lost in woods. She should leave a trail so she could find her way back to Ish and the boat—not breadcrumbs that birds would eat, but white pebbles to shine in the moonlight. Or unravel a ball of string as she walked . . .

She had nothing like that.

She made do with whatever she found at each turn—a crow feather, a clump of bright yellow lichen, three twigs to make the shape of an arrow on the snow. Her own tracks would guide her back.

She kept on walking in the same direction: north-west. She could tell the direction by looking at the trees: the way the snow clung more to one side of the tree than the other. On the way back she'd need to walk south-east, using the snow on the sides of the trees to guide her.

She wished she'd agreed a signal with Ish—a warning cry, like an owl hoot, that they could both make if there was any danger. People about. Gunshot. Guards.

The fir trees were thinning out. The snow fell steadily, blotting out the sky. There was just the faintest glimmer low in the west. It must be mid-afternoon. An hour or so till nightfall. She did not want to be alone in the wood after dark.

The woodland trees were different here—no longer the dark conifers with dry pine needles and barren soil beneath. There was deeper snow, covering dead brambles and clumps of grass and moss. She knew the names of these trees: gnarled oak and smooth grey ash, the best for firewood; prickly holly and the wild bushy hazel trees which at one time would have been coppiced and thinned to make fences and posts and bean sticks for the grand gardens. Only the holly trees kept their leaves in winter: the rest were bare skeletons.

It smelled different, too—of damp, decaying leaves, and mud and bog and something sharp and rank: the stink where a fox had marked its territory.

Ahead, she glimpsed the stones of a tumbledown wall covered in ivy and the grey fluff of wild clematis seeds— old man's beard. She waded on through the deep snow.

The wall marked the edge of the old garden. Bonnie climbed over it.

The house had tumbled further into ruin. The upstairs rooms had been exposed to the weather over many years. Paint and old wallpaper had peeled away to the plaster beneath. The staircase had rotted away. No way could you go up there.

The rooms on the ground floor offered a bit more shelter. Bonnie stepped over a pile of rubble into what must have once been the kitchen. The stone chimney and fireplace were still mostly intact.

She walked through the doorway into the next room and gasped.

A massive painting of a girl filled the entire wall, floor to ceiling. The girl had long dark hair, and hazel eyes and dark lashes, and she was lying on a meadow of grass and daisies. In one hand she held a huge golden dandelion flower. In the other, the seed head of a dandelion flower turned to fluff. She was blowing the seeds, like Bonnie had done when she was little, to make a wish and to tell the time. A dandelion clock.

The painting was minutely detailed, so you could see every petal, every grass blade, each eyelash. Sun and rain and wind over years had cracked the plaster and rubbed away some of the colour and crazed the surface. The girl's blue and gold patterned dress looked vaguely familiar—from a picture in one of Granda's art books, maybe. Bonnie stared in wonder. Who would have painted something so powerful and beautiful in a ruined house in the middle of the woods?

An artist, that's who. Someone brave. Bold.

Five graffiti words outlined in black and filled in with yellow paint splashed over another wall:

LOVE FREEDOM JUSTICE PEACE BEAUTY

Bonnie wandered through the empty rooms searching for more paintings, but there were none. There was another big fireplace and chimney in the room next to the one with the mural. In the rest of the house, ash and elder saplings and baby holly trees had taken root in cracks in the walls. Snow lay in drifts where once would have been carpets and polished wooden floors. Gradually, nature was taking back the house and the gardens and turning them wild again.

A flock of black rooks took off from one of the tall trees beyond the ruined house. They circled above the tree, and landed back among the bare branches. They cackled and clucked to each other as they settled again.

Bonnie wrinkled up her nose. The house smelled of damp and rot. No way Ish could stay here for long. He'd freeze to death.

The snow had stopped. The clouds began to clear.

Dark

Bonnie was used to the dark. It was an everyday part of her life—there was no electric at Granda's and only candles and lanterns for light in winter. But this dark was different. What was it hiding? Who might be out there?

At first, the trees' bare branches allowed the late afternoon light to filter through and Bonnie found her own tracks easily enough to retrace her steps. But the light faded fast. Now, she was surrounded by pine and fir trees. They had been planted so close to each other that the evergreen canopy shut out any last light in the sky. The trees seemed to close in around her. It was hard to see anything. She tripped twice and grazed her knees on stones hidden under the snow. She lost the trail of her own footsteps: more snow had fallen and covered them up. When she stopped and listened, the silence folded around her thick and deep. She dared not call out to Ish in case someone else was out there, listening. Armed guards. A runaway man.

Something scurried in the branches above and sent a shower of snow cascading onto her back. A squirrel or a bird, most likely, but it still made Bonnie's skin twitch. She walked on, searching for signs of her own boot tracks, or the markers she'd left, but she found nothing.

Something pale and ghostly glided between the dark trees on silent wings. Barn owl. Bonnie stopped to watch. Granda had explained to her how an owl could see so well in the dark because of its huge eyes, and special cells at the back of the eye called rods, thousands of them, many more than a human eye, and a sort of mirror that reflects any available light.

Granda. Tears welled up. He was alone in the house, with his hacking cough, full of worry about her. What if the Border Guards had already searched the house and found her missing, when she was supposed to be ill at home? What would they do to Granda?

Bonnie took a deep breath.

Granda. What would he say to her, if he were here now?

Let your eyes adjust. You can see more than you think you can. Take your time. Patience. There's no hurry, Bonnie. Be methodical. Trust yourself.

Get your bearings. Use common sense. Look around for natural navigation signs.

His voice was inside her head, calming her down.

Golden lichens like the south side of a tree . . .

Snow will stick more on the north-east side . . .

She began to find a direction, and as if to help her, a thin sickle moon appeared and lit the snow enough for her to slowly pick her way south-east.

She stopped to listen again. She'd heard something—the call of wild geese, it sounded like. It was coming from the direction where the lake would be if she'd calculated right. Good.

She kept going. She let the words of a song tumble in her head in rhythm with her feet. *Speed bonnie boat, like a bird on the wing.* She'd loved it ever since she was a little girl, because it had her name, Bonnie, in the words.

And another:

My Bonnie lies over the ocean,
My Bonnie lies over the sea,
My Bonnie lies over the ocean,
O bring back my Bonnie to me.

Ahead of her through the trees, she spotted something. A faint light, flickering in the dark. She stopped. Waited. It stayed in the same place. She walked silently on.

Ish sat in the boat, the blanket wrapped around him, the stub of beeswax candle perched on the edge sending its tiny light out to guide her.

'Thank goodness!' Bonnie almost hugged him. 'I thought I'd never get back to you again!'

'You find the house?'

'Yes.'

Ish blew out the candle. 'Walk now. Too cold for sitting.'

Bonnie nodded. 'Sorry I was so long.'

'Is far?'

'About a mile. It'll take us half an hour, maybe more. It'll be much slower dragging the boat.'

Bonnie was tired. She'd have rested for a while had Ish not been so keen to get moving. But it made sense to get him hidden, and then she'd have the long walk back home, by herself in the dark all over again.

As the sky cleared, the temperature dropped. The new layer of snow froze hard. Pale mist flowed between the dark trees. Bonnie's hands were numb with cold, even with gloves.

Ish pulled the cuffs of the woollen jumper over his hands.

They pushed and pulled the boat between them, and neither said a word to break the deep silence of the wood. All they heard was the hiss of the hull of the boat sliding over ice. They followed the trail of Bonnie's boot prints, silver in the moonlight, all the way through the woods to the house.

13

The Ruined House

They left the boat in a corner of the overgrown garden, upturned to keep the inside dry, and covered it with ivy as camouflage.

'Now, let's get you settled inside the house,' Bonnie said.

They climbed over the rubble into the kitchen.

'Sit down here, next to the fireplace.' Bonnie tucked the blanket around Ish. She tried lighting a bundle of twigs and logs, but they smoked and smouldered and gave no heat.

'The wood's too damp. Maybe there's an old cellar somewhere, with leftover coal,' Bonnie said. 'We can have a proper look in the morning.'

Ghostly light from the candle stub threw giant shadows against the flaking plaster on the walls. Ish shivered and shook under the blanket. He looked feverish.

'I have to go now,' Bonnie said. 'I'll bring food and another blanket when I come back tomorrow. More medicine.'

'Stay here,' Ish said.

'I can't,' Bonnie said. 'My granda needs to know I'm safe. I'm sorry. But it's best like this. Just rest. You must stay hidden. No one must know you're here. Understand?'

He nodded. He pulled the blanket over his face.

She looked back once. She could no longer make out the ruined house among the trees. There was no smoke from a fire to give Ish away. The candle had long burned down. Surely no one was going to be tramping through the woods this time of night.

Bonnie picked up a fallen branch of fir, and used it like a broom to sweep the snow smooth behind her as she walked. Just in case.

The sickle moon rose higher in the sky. It was easier than she'd expected to find the way back home. The sky was ablaze with stars.

She stopped at the back door. Voices. A lantern shone at the kitchen window. Someone was there with Granda.

Bonnie listened. A woman's voice rose and fell. A soft laugh.

Granda coughed. The woman said something.

Bonnie waited, unsure what to do. No one had visited Granda for a long time. He used to have friends in the village, though. This person sounded friendly.

It was too cold to wait outside any longer. She opened the door very quietly and slipped inside. The voices were now coming from the front room. Bonnie pulled off her snowy boots and left them neatly by the kitchen stove. She crept through the hall and up the stairs to her room. She left her door open just a crack, so she could listen.

She took off her wet coat and hung it on the hook on the back of the bedroom door. She climbed under the bedcovers, still dressed. An owl hooted; moonlight crept into the room. And still the voices downstairs rose and fell, punctuated by Granda's racking cough.

At last the living room door opened. The woman wished Granda goodnight. Her voice was clear and warm. 'It was good to see you,' she said. 'And the sloe liqueur was a rare and wonderful treat in these troubled times.'

Granda mumbled something.

'I'll bring more linctus in the morning, Matty. And a few extra remedies, to help that terrible chest of yours. Stay warm; rest as much as you can. I shouldn't have kept you up so late.'

The front door opened. Bonnie felt the draught of cold air.

She imagined the woman hugging Granda, blowing him a kiss, perhaps, as she stepped out onto the path at the front of the house and walked back to the village. An old friend from the past, when things had been different. She imagined Granda watching her go.

It seemed a long time before Bonnie heard the click of the front door being shut.

She let out her breath.

'Granda?' she called down.

He coughed and coughed.

Bonnie went to the top of the stairs. 'Granda?'

He looked so little and old and vulnerable, coughing in the hall. Bonnie couldn't bear to see him so frail. She ran down the stairs and put her arms around him and squeezed him tight.

'Oh Bonnie, love,' he said when she finally let him go. 'Thank goodness you're safe back. We had a visitor. I didn't want her to know you weren't here.'

'Who?'

'An old friend. Maggie.'

Bonnie nodded.

'Heard I was ill. Gossip travels, even if people can't go far.' He held her at arm's length, studied her face. 'You're all right, Bonnie? All safe?'

'Yes.'

'The guards came poking around. I wouldn't let them upstairs, and they weren't going to make a thing of it, on account of your infection.' Granda coughed again. 'We had a bit of a job not being able to find the outhouse key and all, but they seemed satisfied I wasn't harbouring any strangers.'

Bonnie took a deep breath. 'But I am. And it's too hard. Too dangerous. I don't know what to do.' There, she'd finally said it.

Granda rested his hand on her head. *Like a blessing,* Bonnie thought later, when she went over everything in her mind.

'You do know. You do what you must do. Your judgements are good, Bonnie. I'm proud of you. Helping others in need. Kindness to strangers. Not following the rules when those rules are wrong-headed or bad.

'But now we both need sleep. We will talk more in the morning.'

14

Thaw

But they didn't talk in the morning. Granda stayed in bed in his room, and Bonnie left him to sleep on while she collected the things she needed. Cheese and bread and apples, beeswax candles, a lantern, a cooking pot, some dry kindling twigs, a blanket off her bed, socks, a pair of waterproof boots that Granda wouldn't miss, just for a day or two, and his small brass compass, to help her find the way back to the ruined house.

She fed the hens and collected four eggs; she hard-boiled them and left one on the kitchen table for Granda's breakfast. *I'll be out all day*, she scribbled on a scrap of paper. She was glad she'd heard Granda's friend say she'd be calling in to see him today.

She wrapped the other three eggs in a clean cloth. She bundled everything into the big canvas bag Granda and she used when it was apple harvest time, and set off back to the woods.

The air smelled different this early morning. A pale sun rose above the trees in the eastern sky. The snow underfoot was softer, wetter. Bonnie felt different too. Lighter inside. Someone was helping Granda. Ish would be on his way soon, now his leg was healing. Her life would go back to . . .

She stopped. She didn't want to go *back*.

High in the sky above the woodland trees, a single buzzard circled, wings outstretched. Bonnie could see the fanned pinion feathers at the tips of the wings. The bird cried, a mewing, melancholy sound. And as if in answer, the flock of geese on the lake called to each other, a chorus of different voices.

Bonnie tried to imagine what it would be like to be able to soar and float like the buzzard, free and high above this place. To travel huge distances like the migrating geese. Her mind wandered to the atlas, those pages of maps, all the places in the wide world that were waiting to be explored. Places different from her own little world. Her own mother, out there somewhere.

She walked on. She didn't need the compass: she could use the sun to guide her.

She caught the faint whiff of woodsmoke. She clambered over the tumbledown garden wall and hurried towards the house.

Ish was sitting by a small fire in the old kitchen.

'Great! You found some dry wood.' Bonnie dumped the heavy bag on the floor. 'Best keep the fire small, so no one sees the smoke.'

'Yes. I find pump too. I wash all over in freezing cold water! My leg is much better. I clean it.' He stretched it out to show her. He'd removed the bandage. The wound was pink where new skin was growing, but the puffiness had gone down.

Everything about Ish looked better. His eyes were brighter, his face more lively.

'That's really good, Ish. Now, breakfast. Or did you *find* that, too?'

Ish frowned. 'How?'

He didn't understand she was teasing him. 'Well, you found wood, and you found water. I thought you might have found a whole larder full of food!'

Ish shook his head.

Bonnie handed him an egg, and a hunk of bread and

cheese, and sat down next to him by the fire while he stuffed the food down in hungry mouthfuls.

'I brought you these. Granda won't miss them for the next few days, and I thought you needed them more.' She took the boots out of the bag.

Ish put them on. He wriggled his toes around. 'These very good boots. Dry feet at last. Thank you!'

She rummaged in the bag for the pan. 'We can use this to boil water on the fire, for drinking. Don't drink water straight from the pump, Ish. It might make you sick again.'

He smiled. 'Too late. But is good water, fresh.'

'Well maybe it's from a spring like we have at home. They'd have needed one, back when people lived here.'

'Who live here?' Ish asked.

'No one, for years.'

'I find dead people stones.'

Bonnie frowned. 'What do you mean?'

'I show you.'

He limped to the far edge of the garden, and called her over. 'Come and see. Stones with names.'

Beyond the wall under the shade of a yew tree she saw the row of small gravestones covered in moss and lichen and ivy. They reminded Bonnie of the stones in the long grass around the disused church in the village, from the old days, before the rule that dead people must be burned, not buried, to stop any risk of spreading disease. Except, these gravestones were much smaller, barely up to her knee. Perhaps they were for babies or children who had died.

Ish climbed over the wall. He rubbed away the snow and some of the moss and lichen. He peeled back the strands of ivy.

Letters, words had been carved roughly into the surface of the stones as if by a child or someone not used to using stone-carving tools. Rain and sun and wind over many years had worn away some of the words completely.

Bonnie climbed over the wall and stood next to him. She read aloud the names she could make out:

MITTENS, WHO LOVED THE SUN
PIPPI, TRUSTED FRIEND
ORLANDO, DEARLY MISSED
PILOT, BELOVED DOG

'They're the graves for *animals*,' Bonnie said. 'Pets like cats and dogs who died. The family must have buried them here.'

Ish smoothed his hand across the carved letters. He sounded out the names.

Pilot. She'd heard that name before.

Yes! It came to her: the dog in the photograph of Mam on the beach. *Pilot* was the dog that had belonged to the lad from the big house.

Aidan.

Her mam's friend, who grew up to be the man who was maybe the father of the baby who died. Fritha.

All the pieces slotted into place.

This was the big house! Aidan had lived here, before it had been abandoned and fallen into ruin.

Had Aidan painted the mural of the girl?

She remembered the little drawings in Mam's letters in fine pen and ink.

Aidan was an artist? It was possible . . .

Ish was watching her. 'You OK?' he asked.

She nodded. 'I just realized something. The family that once lived in this house, well, one of the sons was called Aidan, and he knew my mam, and they had a baby, my sister Fritha.' She stopped. The words *my sister* sounded so weird.

Ish was trying to understand. 'Your family live here?'

'No, my mam's boyfriend. Ages ago. Before everything

went wrong and she went away. In a boat. And I haven't seen her since I was a baby and maybe she's dead and I can't even remember her.' It all tumbled out.

'Say again, slow.'

Bonnie explained the best she could, about Mam and the baby, and Mam going away to a place where she could live a bigger life with more freedom, leaving Bonnie behind. 'She said she'd come back for me and Granda, but she never did.'

Ish listened. He didn't say anything.

When Bonnie glanced at him she saw tears on his face. Perhaps he was thinking of the people he'd lost, or left behind. She'd seen the pictures he'd drawn. They told his story well enough.

A small bird landed on the yew tree. Robin. It sang its chirpy song. It flew down to the wall and looked at them with its beady eye, as if expecting something. It did not seem afraid. Snow slid off a branch and all around was the sound of dripping foliage. Bonnie sniffed the air. Yes, something had definitely changed.

'The snow's melting,' Bonnie said.

Ish nodded. 'We take boat back to beach tonight,' he said. 'On snow is possible. With no snow, is too heavy to carry so far.'

'And then what? You'll go?'

'Of course.'

'But it's so dangerous—the guards are everywhere, they'll be checking the coast—'

'Here no good for me.' He looked at Bonnie. 'No good for you either.'

'What do you mean?'

'Not happy. Live in fear. Not much food always only eggs.'

That made Bonnie smile. 'It's winter, that's all. In summer we have vegetables from the garden, and fruit, and there's crabs and shrimps and fish sometimes . . .' Her voice petered out.

Ish was right. She wasn't happy. She loved Granda with all her heart, but there was no one else. No one at the horrible school or in the village. And the rules and regulations kept on getting tighter and more rigid. And Granda . . . she blinked back tears. One day, Granda wouldn't be here any more. And then what would her life be like?

'So why did you come here?' Bonnie asked.

'Is by mistake. The wind and sea bring me.'

'Where did you mean to go?'

'North lands, where is lakes and forest and good fish

and people friendly to the stranger. This man, he tell me the place. He helped me with the boat and is very kind. He have sons and daughters too. He understand what it is like to lose your family. Lose everything.'

'Maybe it's the same place where Aidan went—he sent a letter to my mam, about a place like that with lakes and forest—'

Ish grabbed her arm. 'Sshh. Listen!'

Bonnie heard the faint drip of melting snow. And then a thud, and the *crack* of a dead branch breaking.

'What is it?' she whispered.

He pulled her down next to him, behind the wall.

'There's someone at the house.'

15

Runaway

A man, dark-haired, bearded, in dark clothes—that was all Bonnie glimpsed. He was picking through their things—delighted, no doubt, by the discovery of food, and firewood, a blanket, and a house that offered some shelter. Bonnie wanted to run out and tell him to leave their stuff alone. But that would be stupid. Dangerous. He might be armed.

Ish kept his hand on her arm. 'We just wait,' he whispered.

'But what if he stays here? What if he finds the boat?' Bonnie whispered back.

The man wasn't one of the Border Guards—no uniform. Perhaps this was the man the guards had been searching for yesterday. And maybe it was his blood that she'd seen on the snow, and he'd been hiding in the woods all night. Bonnie shivered.

She smelled wood smoke. A plume of it drifted up from the old chimney.

Stupid. That was the quickest way to draw attention to himself. Or maybe he thought he was too well hidden, deep in the woods, and that the Border Guards were miles away. Did he not wonder whose things he'd just been rummaging through? How could he know they weren't a danger to him?

Perhaps he'd been watching her and Ish the whole time. Knew they were children. Unarmed. A chill went down her spine.

Or perhaps he was expecting someone to bring him food . . . had arranged to meet them here . . . Bonnie's imagination began to conjure up all sorts of stories. The man was part of a gang of runaways . . . This was their meeting place . . . they were planning to cross the border at one of the weak points; they'd shoot the guards . . . Or maybe he was totally harmless, like them. Simply wanting a new life beyond borders . . .

'I'm getting cramp,' Bonnie whispered. 'I need to move my legs.'

'Not now! Shhhh!'

The man had come out of the house. He stood in the overgrown garden, looking around.

Bonnie held her breath. Ish tensed up, as if all his energy was focused on stopping himself from running forward.

Any moment now, the man would surely see the boat.

Or them.

Both.

Ish reached out and gradually loosened a stone from the wall. He waited as a series of smaller stones trickled out, then reached again. His fingers tightened around the stone. He lifted it.

Did he mean to throw it? To hit the man?

'No!' she whispered.

The man stepped through the deep snow. He stopped, looked down at his feet, studying something.

Of course! Their footprints were everywhere. She'd not thought to brush them clear and no fresh snow had fallen.

But the man did not come further. He seemed uncertain. He looked nervously about him. He went back to the house. They heard the clatter of the cooking pot being knocked over. Silence followed.

Bonnie shifted position. She stretched out one leg, then the other.

'Maybe he's scared,' she whispered. 'He's realized someone's been here, but he doesn't know it's us. Our footprints—yours are adult-sized.'

'Yes.'

Everything went quiet at the house. No human sounds, just the drip, drip of melting snow, the raucous cawing of rooks in the tall ash tree, other smaller birds: robin and sparrow and wren. Bonnie and Ish settled themselves, backs against the wall, and waited.

Ish had his eyes closed. Maybe he was asleep. They seemed to have been waiting for hours. Bonnie was cold and damp and fidgety.

'He must have gone,' she whispered. 'I'm going to see.'

It was a relief to stand up straight, and to move about. She climbed over the garden wall, crouched down again to wait for any sound, and crept towards the house. There's nothing to be afraid of, she told herself. I've as much right to walk in the woods as anyone else. I'm not a runaway, in hiding.

Phew. The boat was still where they'd left it.

She walked softly round the side of the house and into the kitchen.

The fire had gone out. The cooking pot had gone. The bag with the food and the blanket had gone. The man had taken everything except the rolled-up pictures and the tin of coloured pencils.

Mean, she first thought. And then she understood: *desperate, that's all.* Or maybe he'd thought the things had been left there for him by a kind stranger, or a fellow freedom seeker. Was this some secret meeting place, even?

Bonnie wandered through the empty rooms. The massive painted girl in the mural seemed to watch Bonnie with her big, kind eyes.

Outside, the rooks took off with loud shrieks, as if suddenly alarmed.

Bonnie stood still to listen.

Voices. Men's voices. Heavy footsteps. The stamping of boots.

She whirled round, looking for a place to hide. She ran through the doorway into the next room. There was no more time. The voices were coming closer. She squeezed herself into a space inside the big fireplace and hunkered down, heart hammering.

The voices got louder. Now they were right in the room next door.

A rough laugh. 'Look at this muck!' A man read out aloud the graffiti words in a mocking voice. '*Peace! Love! Freedom!*'

'Must be their meeting place. Freedom Headquarters!'

Gunshots rang out, deafeningly loud.

Bonnie ducked, hands over her ears. Could bullets go through stone?

Plaster and loose stone trickled down the wall.

She heard another voice, a young man it sounded like. Excited, enjoying the hunt. 'He's been here! Kitchen fire's still warm. He's left a pile of crazy drawings.'

Someone laughed, a mocking, horrible sound.

'Any clues?'

She couldn't hear what was said next.

The fireplace smelled of stone dust. Ancient soot. She gulped breaths, prayed she wouldn't sneeze, that they would come no further.

'Gone which way you reckon?' The young man's voice, reedy and clear.

'Through the woods, further up the border.'

'He won't make it.'

'No chance.'

Bonnie heard the crackling sound of a radio; muffled

voices and footsteps as the men went back out. Laughter. Someone swore.

The men crashed through the trees, joking and swearing.

The voices grew fainter.

Finally silence folded back in.

The rooks returned to the tall tree.

Faint gunshot echoed once from deep in the woods.

Please let them not find that poor man. Keep him safe.

She was glad the runaway man had taken their food, now. She wished him safe passage. Sanctuary.

At last she felt safe enough to squeeze herself out of the hiding space. She crossed the empty room and went through the doorway.

Oh! She blinked back tears. The beautiful mural was spattered with shot.

It was as if the Border Guards had wanted to wound or kill the girl, destroy everything lovely, wipe out the words of peace and love and justice and freedom.

'Bonnie! Bonnie?'

Ish was calling her. It was the first time she'd heard him actually say her name. It was comforting to hear her name spoken aloud in this place of ruin.

'Here!' she called back.

Ish stood in the doorway.

'Bonnie! You are OK?' he asked. 'I worry when hear shootings. I feel bad I not come to help you.'

'Horrid, violent, ignorant men. I hid in the fireplace next door, just in time. But look what they did in here.'

Ish stared at the bullet holes. He shook his head. 'Terrible, to destroy beautiful things. Why?'

'I don't understand, either,' Bonnie said. 'What's the matter with people like that? Why are they so full of hate?'

Ish and Bonnie stared at the destruction in silence.

Bonnie turned away. 'But at least they didn't search properly. Didn't see the boat. And they've gone. So, we're lucky, really.'

'So now we go.'

'In daylight?'

'Yes, is much too dangerous here. We take boat to beach. Now.'

There was hardly anything left to pack up. Ish rolled up the paper and gathered up the scattered coloured pencils.

Bonnie crouched down to help.

'Oh!' Someone had scribbled on the plaster at the edge of the fireplace in yellow pencil. A single word in tiny letters—*Pilgrim*—and a spiky circle a bit like a dandelion flower. The runaway man must have done it—a sign that he had been there, leaving his mark.

'Come on. Hurry!' Ish was already outside, working the boat free from the tangle of ivy.

Together they began to push the boat through the slushy garden.

Beach

The beach.

Most of the snow had melted from the sand. The sea was a deep grey, like solid metal. It smelled strongly of salt, and rotting weed, and something so rank it made Bonnie's nose itch. The tide was high.

They pushed the boat into the dunes and stopped at last.

Bonnie rested her weary arms.

They hadn't even stopped when they got to Bonnie's house. Ish said there was no time. Bonnie had wanted to get more food and a blanket for Ish to take on his voyage, but every second it would take for her to get stuff, and to talk to Granda, was a second they could not afford. The

Border Guards seemed to be everywhere. For the last part of the journey, when they were close to the village, they had heard the constant roar of armoured vehicles going up the hill, and the tramp of boots, and once they thought they heard something in the sky—a drone or even an ancient plane, if such a thing were possible, though they never actually saw it.

Why did one runaway man cause such alarm? Unless there were more people on the run . . . Perhaps he was part of a bigger group making a bid for freedom. Or maybe the man was someone important, someone who would cause trouble for the guards, a political leader or an enemy . . .

He hadn't looked important. He had looked frail and hungry and afraid.

It was as well that the footpath had been piled so high with snow—each night it had re-frozen, so that over many days and nights it had packed down to solid ice. Once they'd got through the trees and out of the wood, the boat had slid easily enough. And it was lucky that so few village people used the old footpaths, or came to the beach in winter. They could see no point. They believed the stories about the sea being deadly dangerous. Few people knew which shellfish or weeds were good to eat. The great poisoning of the oceans had made most people scared. And the wealthy people did not think fish was a worthy food: they turned their backs to the sea and looked to the land instead.

Bonnie surveyed the coast anxiously, north and south. She'd been afraid there would be armed guards down here on the beach itself, or a ship patrolling the shore. And when she screwed her eyes against the light, she could see something, away to the north: a grey patrol boat.

'It's too dangerous to leave now,' she told Ish. 'The patrol guards will have binoculars and stuff. You must wait for nightfall. Aim for the islands; you can stay there the rest of the night, or as long as you want, till the weather is right for a longer journey. You can shelter in the house of light. Catch fish. There might be a well, for water. The guards won't go near the island, because of the deaths there. Poisoned soil. It's still in quarantine. But Granda says that's just fearmongering: it's not true.'

Ish frowned. He unstrapped the oars from under the seat of the boat. He untied the rope, coiled it and stowed it at the bow.

Her rope.

Bonnie gulped back a sob: she'd thought of it as *her boat*, too, and now it was going away, and all her chances of new life and hope and travel and maybe finding her own mam were going too. And Ish would be gone forever.

Her new friend, Ish.

Did he guess what she was thinking? He put the oars ready, checked the rowlocks, examined the bottom of the boat for leaks. 'You come too,' he said, without looking at her.

'How?' she said. 'It's not possible. Granda . . .'

A series of images flashed through her mind. Granda coughing. Granda dozing by the fire in the evening. Granda sleeping late in the morning, ill and old.

Granda, who had raised her since she was a tiny baby, who had loved her and looked after her and taught her and made her everything she was.

But Granda's voice came into her head, very clear and calm.

Go. Live your life. This is your chance for a bigger, better life than you can have here. Take it. Go. Create a better world. This is what I have raised you to do, Bonnie.

Ish was already pushing the boat through the dunes and onto the sand. He tried to lift it over the stones at the top of the beach but he was not strong enough.

Bonnie ran to help. Together they carried the boat over the stones and set it afloat in the shallow water.

Ish climbed into the boat. He settled himself on the seat, back to the sea. He picked up an oar in each hand.

Bonnie waded into the shallow water ready to give the boat one final shove. Even through her boots, she felt how cold the sea was.

'Now I go,' Ish said. 'And you?' He put his hand in his pocket, drew out the small leather button Bonnie had given him. *Mam's* button, from her sheepskin coat. He held it out. 'You should have,' he said. 'If you not come.'

She looked back at the land. A single grey goose was flying steadily north-eastward, neck outstretched, calling softly. From somewhere near the village, a plume of black smoke rose into the sky. The acrid smell of burnt cloth wafted over the water.

The goose was a sign.

'I want to come with you, I do. More than anything. But I cannot leave Granda behind. He needs me.' Her eyes filled with tears.

Ish nodded. 'I understand. Is your family.'

Bonnie could not bear it. She sobbed as if her heart would break. She had this one chance of freedom. She might not get another . . .

Ish sculled the boat parallel to the shore. He used one

oar to anchor it in the shallow water. 'Listen, stop crying,' he said. 'Go, fetch your granda, come fast as you can. We bring him with us, yes?'

Bonnie stared. 'You mean that? You'll really wait? You'll take us both?'

Ish nodded. 'Be quick. If anyone come, I must row away, but I return when safe. Maybe when dark. Stay on beach. Yes? Now run!'

Would he wait? Was it simply a way to get rid of her, because he'd changed his mind about her? Bonnie's thoughts bounced around her head. She was out of breath; her legs shook, she'd never run so fast. What was the right way to persuade Granda? How would she get him to come straight away? There was no time to prepare properly for a journey . . .

A distant volley of shots echoed from somewhere inland. Maybe the Border Guards had caught up with the fugitive man . . . maybe other people were on the run. Bonnie stopped to catch her breath, heart hammering.

It seemed strangely quiet just here: there was no sound of engines, no raised voices coming from the village. The drama—the shooting, or whatever it was—

was happening elsewhere. Good. It gave them a little extra time.

Granda was standing at the open door. He had his coat on, his canvas haversack at his feet. No boots.

'I saw you go down the path.' His voice wobbled. 'You and the stranger boy and the beautiful boat. And you know I want for you to be free, Bonnie, but I wished I had said goodbye. I thought to come to the beach, to see you go.'

'I'm not going without you. The boy is waiting at the beach for us. We have to hurry. You have to come with me. Now.'

He looked impossibly old and frail, standing there in his socks, his lined face wet with tears.

She'd stolen his warm boots and given them to Ish . . .

He'd thought she had left him without saying goodbye . . .

'You're coming with me.' She used her fiercest voice. 'I'll get your shoes. There's no time for anything else.'

She helped lace up his old leather shoes. She found his gloves and hat and scarf and wrapped him up as warm as she could. She grabbed the warm bread loaf from the rack on the kitchen table, and shoved it in his bag. 'Now we must go fast as we can.'

Granda did not resist. 'There's nothing for me here. I am an old, old man,' he said over and over, as Bonnie locked the door and helped him down the garden path. She had to hold his arm to stop him slipping on the melting snow.

'I nearly forgot the hens!' she gasped, when they got to the gate, and she ran back to the shed and opened the door so the hens could find their own way outside to forage and find water. She'd give them their own chance of freedom.

Granda was so slow! It was agony to Bonnie how slowly he stumbled along, even though he was leaning on her, so she was half carrying him along the slippery footpath to the beach. When had he got so weak? Had this been happening for months without her noticing? He was light as a feather.

Each precious minute they took meant it less likely that Ish would still be waiting.

Granda was gasping for breath. They stopped and he coughed and spat and took shallow gulps of air. 'You go on,' he wheezed. 'I am a very foolish, fond old man. You're better off without me now, Bonnie. I'm holding you back.'

'Don't be silly. I need you. You need me. We go together.'

Granda barely had strength to smile. But his weary face did light up when at last they got to the dunes, and he saw the sea. 'Oh,' he whispered. 'I'd almost forgotten. Air and space and freedom.'

Bonnie was jittery. Where was the boat?

'Stay here a moment,' Bonnie said. 'Lean on the concrete blocks while I look for Ish.'

Far to the north, the grey patrol boat was in the same place as before, not moving. That was good. There was no one on the beach, as far as she could see.

Had Ish gone without her?

She strained her eyes. A sea fret was moving in, white mist spreading in a layer over the water. And while she watched, she heard the faint creaking sound of a moving boat, and the dip of oars through water, and Ish rowed out from behind the Whin Sill rocks.

Sea Fret

Granda sat hunched in the bow of the boat, his bony hands gripping the sides to keep himself upright. His face was ashen, his mouth set. His eyes seemed to be closed. Just getting into the boat had exhausted him. Granda had nodded to Ish, and pointed to his feet and half-smiled. 'Nice boots, eh!' That was the only thing he'd said.

Bonnie watched him anxiously from her seat in the stern.

What had she done?

The air was ice-cold. The sea fret was swirling in fast. Bonnie pulled up the collar of Mam's sheepskin coat. Ish rowed with all his strength, but the boat seemed to move so slowly. She had no idea how long it would take to reach the island with the house of light. Maybe it wasn't even there. Maybe it was all just a story. She sank further down inside the coat. Everything was sopping wet from the mist and spray. Granda's bad chest would get even worse.

She'd never been in a boat before in her life. Setting off in a miserable small rowing boat on a freezing winter day, putting Granda into real danger . . . had she made a terrible mistake?

Be brave, she told herself, *like Mam*.

The water was choppy. They were moving against the tide. Wave after wave lifted then dropped the little boat. Over and over Bonnie thought how incredible it was that the boat stayed afloat. There was only the thin wooden skin of the boat between them and the depths of the ocean. And what would happen if the boat turned over? She had never learned to swim. Granda would surely drown.

The boat moved in rhythm with the beat of the oars—a lunge forward, then a pause like a breath before the next lunge. If Ish rested the oars for even the shortest time, the boat was dragged back by the tide.

She glanced back to the land for the millionth time.

This time, she thought she saw someone on the headland. A girl in a dark coat, with long dark hair. It was hard to be sure, with the mist coming and going. When she next checked, there was no one there. Even so, it filled Bonnie's heart with dread. If the girl had seen them she might tell the guards, and they'd send out the border patrol boat, and that would be the end of everything.

Bonnie leant forward so Ish could hear her. 'We're being watched.'

'Guards?' Ish glanced up.

'No, a girl.'

'Maybe she one like us,' Ish said. 'Looking for a way to leave.'

'Even so . . .' Bonnie glanced at the blisters on Ish's hands. 'Should I help row? I could try . . . we might be faster.'

'No is too hard. But later I teach you.' He looked over his shoulder. 'Your job now is navigate. Tell me which way to islands.'

'It's impossible to see,' Bonnie said. 'The mist is getting thicker all the time.'

Ish nodded. 'But mist is our friend; keep us hidden too.'

Bonnie felt sick. She'd never really thought about tides and currents and how to find the way in a sea fret. For a while, a flock of black-and-white seabirds flew beside them, as if encouraging them on, and then they too flew away, leaving them alone on the cold grey water, the mist closing in around them. Droplets of moisture beaded her hair and face and coat. The cold went deep, right down into her bones. The mist seemed to swallow up all sound.

Ish hunched over the oars, his head bowed, his face set. On he rowed, steady, slow, determined.

Bonnie sang the words of an old song. It helped keep her courage up.

'Speed bonnie boat, like a bird on the wing
Over the sea to Skye . . .'

Bonnie knew that *Skye* was a real island, but when she sang the word, in her mind she saw an actual blue sky.

In the front of the boat, Granda mouthed the words along with her, even though he had no breath left for singing.

'It's as if we're the only people left in the entire world,' Bonnie said. 'Or as if we've rowed over the edge of the world into nothing.'

Neither Granda nor Ish answered her. Both were saving their breath, she supposed.

She lost all sense of time.

The mist was thick and ghost-white, the sea a strange, glassy grey. The boat seemed to drift through time and space, and the only sound was the creak of the oars.

Bonnie's thoughts drifted too. Everything seemed dreamlike.

A boatman rowing across water.

That was from an old story Granda told her.

And in that ancient story the boatman ferried the dead across a river, didn't he? She tried to remember, but she was so cold, her brain wouldn't work; she needed to sleep.

Perhaps they would never get to the island. They would row on like this forever. Perhaps this was what it was like to die: a kind of dreaminess, a drifting away, the desire to sleep forever.

Letting go of the world.

She closed her eyes. The movement of the boat lulled her. She had let go of her old world now. There was no going back. She was travelling forward into the unknown, towards something new.

This was what she had wanted all along.

Finding the boat, helping Ish: it had all been for this..

A new sound.

Bird calls.

Bonnie opened her eyes. Birds meant they were near some kind of land.

Islands? So, they were real after all . . .

For a moment, the sea fret thinned. Seabirds circled and dived ahead.

'I can see something: rocks, a shadowy cliff. It's the first of the islands!' She felt the thrill of seeing land at last. 'Almost there.'

Ish was exhausted. Numb with cold. He lost grip of one oar and it clattered into the boat.

Bonnie reached forward to grab it, but the sudden movement unbalanced the boat. It rocked alarmingly and she sat back down fast.

Ish shook his head.

The first island reared above them with its high cliffs and rocky inlets. There was nothing but bare rock and screaming seabirds. No shelter.

A sudden sick dread swamped her. What if the stories about death and poison and toxic land were true, after all?

'Not this one,' Bonnie said. 'There's nothing here.'

Bonnie peered anxiously ahead. She held on tight to the sides of the boat, wedged her feet firmly under the seat, called out directions. In the bows, Granda had slumped as if he had fallen asleep.

'Nearly there, Granda,' Bonnie called.

He moved his hand to show her he had heard.

They passed through a narrow channel where the sea was dark and the cliffs loomed high either side. Bonnie shivered. The sea churned and frothed. She would be sick if it kept on like this much longer.

The next two islands came into view through the fog. A stone wall next to a stone tower.

'This is it!' Bonnie called above the slap of water. 'Look, Granda! Like in the old stories!'

Ish rested the oars. The small boat rocked on the swell. 'Is there a landing place?' he asked.

'There must be,' Bonnie said. 'People lived here in the olden days. The light keepers had a boat.'

Ish lifted the oars again.

'Yes! I can see it!' she yelled. 'A small beach and a jetty. Turn left. I mean, your right.'

'Starboard,' Ish said. 'Port left, starboard right.'

'Whatever. We're almost there.'

There was no sight of the mainland they had left behind. It seemed like a lifetime ago already.

The sea fret had saved them. No one could have seen them aim for this island, and no one would see them go ashore. For now, they would be safe.

The boat bobbed more gently in the shelter of the

island. Ish rowed them to stone steps at the beach side of the concrete jetty.

Bonnie stood up. 'My legs are wobbly!'

Granda smiled weakly. 'You'll need to get your sea legs.'

'Shall I help you up?' Bonnie asked him.

'I'll just sit here a moment longer,' Granda said. 'Gather me stiff bones.'

Bonnie clambered past him, up onto the step.

Ish threw her the rope. 'Tie us up on the mooring ring. A good, strong knot. But leave lots of slack, for when the tide goes down.'

Bonnie tied the best knot she could.

'There. Now your turn to go ashore, Granda.' Between them, Bonnie and Ish managed to haul and push Granda out of the boat and up the steps.

It was hard work for everyone. He needed to rest again at the top of the jetty. 'It's OK,' he told Bonnie. 'I'll have a sit-down on that nice flat rock. I can make my own slow way up the slope. You go on, lass.'

'Sure? You warm enough? I'll come back to help you.'

She ran ahead. She couldn't wait to see inside the house of light.

House of Light

Bonnie pushed open the rotten wooden gate into the walled garden and ran up the stone path to the front door. She had imagined a moment like this since she was a little girl, when Granda had first told her the stories about a family who lived in the island house with its neat vegetable garden for fresh food, who kept a light burning in the tower every night to warn passing ships of the dangerous rocks, and had rescued shipwrecked sailors and fisherfolk. She'd imagined a whole tower built of glass, full of light, not this solid stone building with glass only at the very top.

She pushed the wooden door. She tried to turn the handle, but the door was locked. Where might someone leave a key?

She knelt, feeling with her hand under the loose stones of the path. Her fingers grasped cold metal.

An iron key was attached with string to a small cardboard tag. Two words had been beautifully handwritten in faded brown ink: *Lighthouse, front.*

The key turned smoothly in the lock, as if it had been recently oiled and used. The door swung open and Bonnie stepped inside.

Her eyes adjusted to the gloom. Everything was in shadow except for a pale column of daylight shining directly down the centre of a wooden spiral staircase. It made a small pool on the ground floor. Dust motes spun in the light. Bonnie stepped into the pool of light and looked up, up, up. The stairs wound up four or five storeys at least. This room at the bottom was nothing more than an entrance hall. Now she saw hooks for coats, and an ancient doormat made of rough sisal. Switches on the wall, a metal box. She started to climb.

The first floor room was a circular kitchen, everything made to fit perfectly against the round walls. Bonnie ran her hands over the wooden cupboards. She pulled out drawers, and found old-fashioned knives and forks and spoons with bone handles. The cupboard shelves held cups and bowls and plates, solid china, white. There was a solid cast iron stove with places to heat a kettle and another pot on top. There were wooden shutters on the walls, and when she opened them she found narrow, deep-set windows. She peered out. Ish must be down there, still fiddling with the boat, checking her knots or something. She'd go back for Granda soon, when he'd got his breath back.

She opened the doors of another cupboard. She found an old tin with a green lid, and something rattled inside when she shook it. She untwisted the lid. Inside was a packet of oat biscuits—ancient, but they smelled alright when she opened the packet. She nibbled one: salty, dry. She put it in her pocket.

She delved deeper in the cupboard. Tins, lots of them, smaller than the biscuit tin, and sealed up so she'd need a sharp knife to open them. The labels had been eaten away years ago by mice or insects or simply damp and air. But it was obviously food of some kind, enough to keep them going for days, weeks even.

What else would she find?

She climbed on up.

A sitting room next, with soft couches fitted around the edge of the room, and a round wooden table, and wooden glass-fronted bookcases. Bonnie scanned the titles of the books on the shelves: *A History of the Lighthouse; A Natural Philosophy; Palgrave's Golden Treasury of Poetry; Birds of the Northern Hemisphere; The Maintenance and Upkeep of Domestic Fowl; Traditional Boats of the North-East* . . . Different books, ones Granda didn't have, that she'd not seen or read before.

Bonnie was too excited to stay still for long. She climbed on up the spiral stairs and found the bedrooms: two, each with two narrow beds with folded blankets and a washbasin and a china jug for hot water, and higher up, a smaller one with just one bed. She imagined lying there tonight, cosy and safe, at the top of the tower. Bliss!

The higher she climbed, the smaller the rooms. Now she was at the top of the spiral staircase, and she climbed up a final ladder out onto a wooden platform, with nothing but a thin dome of glass between her and the reeling sky. In the middle was the huge lamp itself. Its glass and mirrors reflected back the daylight, but when it was lit it would have sent out its own light, reflected and amplified by all the mirrors and glass to make a light bright enough for passing ships to see. The lamp turned, she remembered Granda telling her, so that the light would seem to flash, and the pattern and rhythm of the flashes was like a message, a code to sailors to tell them where exactly they were.

'Bonnie?' Ish's voice echoed up the stairwell.

'Come up!' she called back. Her voice bounced off the walls, echoed and repeated. *Up up-p . . .*

'It's like being on top of the world!' Bonnie told him when he finally appeared. 'Like being a bird in the sky!' She held her arms wide and spun slowly around. 'It's *heavenly!*' She smiled her biggest smile at Ish's serious face. 'And there's food, and bedding, and everything we need! So what's the matter?'

Ish sighed. 'It doesn't feel right. Is too clean, too perfect.'

'What do you mean?'

'Is like everything is ready for someone. Like someone else is expected. Someone is here before. Recently. Maybe here even now.'

Bonnie stopped spinning.

The key. The oiled lock. The dust-free cupboards. The stack of tinned food. Bedding.

Ish was right. It was all too convenient. They were clearly not the first people to have come here recently.

'There was no other boat at the jetty,' she said. 'You could only get here if you had a boat.'

Ish nodded. He sat down on the wooden floor and rested his head on his hands. He closed his eyes.

Bonnie saw how exhausted he was.

'Thank you for rowing all that way,' she whispered. 'I'm sorry I wasn't much help.'

'Is OK. It balances,' he mumbled. 'You help me, I help you.'

'Yes. So, now you have a sleep on one of those soft beds, and I'll go and help Granda and soon as he's comfortable I'll explore the island. I'll check there's no one hidden. No other boats.'

'Be careful, yes?'

'Of course.'

She followed him down. She helped spread the blanket over him on one of the beds, and then she stepped happily down the rest of the spiral staircase to the bottom.

She stood in the open doorway. The rocky island seemed to float in the mist. She could see a short distance over grey sea flecked with white, and beyond that was nothing but mist in any direction.

The world they'd left had disappeared completely.

Granda hadn't moved.

Bonnie hugged him. 'The house of light is wonderful, Granda! There's beds and a stove and food and everything we need. Books, too. You'll soon get warm and cosy. Come on.' She helped him stand, and waited while he coughed and coughed.

'I should have come earlier,' Bonnie said. 'You've got too cold.'

'No,' Granda said, 'I wanted to sit in the open and take it all in. The sense of being free, in a new place. Moving on. 'Tis wonderful, Bonnie.'

He coughed again, and Bonnie heard the rattle deep in his lungs.

'Lean on me,' she told him. 'We'll go slow and steady up the slope.'

She got him as far as the sitting room, slow step by slow step, and helped him onto the couch. She fetched down a blanket from one of the beds and wrapped it round Granda best she could. He kept his coat and scarf and hat on.

'I'll soon be just grand,' he said. 'I'll close my eyes for a few minutes.'

'You'd be more comfortable on one of the beds on the next floor up,' Bonnie said.

'No, this will be just fine. No more stairs for me for a while. I've not the puff.'

'I'm going to run round the island and check everything's alright. I won't be long. Ish is sleeping. You're sure you're OK?'

Granda patted her hand. 'I'm canny,' he said.

He'd closed his eyes and was snoring even before Bonnie had set foot on the first stair down.

19

Island

The island was like a world in miniature. There were no trees, but there was the walled garden with a well for spring water, the stone house of light, the old jetty and the sandy beach, old footpaths, a ruined stone building that might once have been a chapel. The flat top of the island was a patchwork of grass and snow, as if only light snow had fallen here during all the last wintry weeks. Bonnie ran down the steep stone path to check there were no other boats and that theirs was safely tied up. All was well.

She let herself imagine the horror of someone stealing the boat, leaving Ish and her and Granda stranded. She ran right around the top of the island, and created a whole story in her head about them living on the island for years, growing food somehow in the garden, finding gulls' eggs to eat, and fishing off the rocks. Eventually someone else would land here, she told herself, and rescue them. By then everything would have changed on the mainland, with no more borders and guards, and she and Granda could go back to the house, and Ish would live with them too and her mam would sail back with Aidan and they would all live happily ever after. That was how stories were supposed to end.

She peered over the cliff. No boats. No way anyone could land on this rocky side of the island. Breaking waves threw flecks of spume up the steep cliffs. White seabirds circled, calling to each other in alarm as she got close. Granda had told her about the birds. In olden times, boats brought people to see the thousands of birds that came to the islands to breed: puffins and Arctic terns, guillemots and razorbills and other seabirds that had disappeared when the sea became poisoned and were only gradually returning. Only the big vicious gulls had thrived, living off the rubbish that people created on the land.

Bonnie walked back to the lighthouse.

No one else was here.

Just her and Granda and Ish.

And it was a safe place, a happy place, after all. Granda had been right about that.

It was funny being the only person awake. She climbed the spiral stairs, past Granda, and up another two flights to check on Ish.

She watched his chest rise and fall with each breath, saw how deeply he slept. His face twitched as if he were dreaming. Once or twice he flung out an arm as if to push something away. He moaned quietly.

Bonnie went back down the stairs to the sitting room and sat down on the couch opposite Granda. She was still too full of energy, a coiled spring. Her mind buzzed. She jumped up and opened the drawers under the glass cabinet with the books. There was a small box of paints and an ink pen. Ish would love those. Maps—sea charts, she supposed, with blue lines and numbers. She opened one out and studied it. Perhaps it would help them find their way, if only she could work out what the lines and numbers meant. She rummaged further into the drawer and discovered a round, brass compass, small enough to rest easily in her palm. She tapped it and watched the arrow swing and she turned the compass around until the arrow pointed magnetic north. Brilliant. She put the compass down on the table and went back to the drawer. She pulled out a paper notebook and a pencil. Someone had written on the second and third pages, scribbled tiny notes and numbers. They didn't make any sense to her either. Was it a code of some kind? A secret message? She gave up trying to work it out and went down to the kitchen.

She took a metal bucket and went outside to the well. It was like the one at home, only this one had a heavy wooden cover and it took ages to shove and heave it off the top. But the water smelled sweet and clean; she dipped the bucket to scoop some up. She would know if it was poisoned, surely?

How to light the stove? She found fuel—charcoal, in a paper sack. She needed the flint striker. She hoped it was safe in Ish's pocket. 'But there's bound to be one here,' Bonnie said aloud, 'because everything is here, ready.' She hunted through the drawers and found a strange tool that magically made a spark when you clicked on a button. She found kindling, too: thin shavings of wood in a box. She made up the fire, lit it, put the kettle on top to heat up. They'd have tea, and water for washing, and open one of the tins for dinner. It was riches beyond her dreams.

But Ish's thought still lingered in her mind: was it all *too* perfect? Was someone else expected?

Granda slept on. Ish slept too. His face looked calmer now, his body no longer thrashing around fighting invisible forces. Bonnie climbed on up the steps to the very top, to the light. Originally it would have been a fire at the open top of the tower, to be kept burning all night. Later it was a light that worked on electricity, Granda said, and then a light powered by the sunlight, though right now it was hard to imagine there was ever enough sun here to make energy for a light.

If it was solar-powered, why had it stopped working? Could it be started up again? Imagine, suddenly the light shining out again! But that would be ridiculous of course: the quickest way possible of drawing attention to themselves.

She peered through the glass panes of the dome. Daylight was fading. The sea crashed onto the rocky islands. More were visible now the tide had gone out. Was the mist thinning a little? Hard to tell; it was getting dark.

For now, they were safe and could rest. Sleep was healing. They'd need all their strength for the journey ahead.

Fear fluttered in her chest. How long would they be at sea? How many days and weeks and how would they ever find the way to a safe haven? Was the boat strong enough? Was Granda?

She thought of the little compass, the arrow flickering with movement, finding north. Aidan had made the crossing. Mam, too. She had to believe it was possible for them to do the same.

Bonnie stepped all the way back down to the bottom of the spiral staircase to the hooks where she'd hung her coat.

She found Aidan's letter to Mam deep in the coat pocket, and smoothed out the creased page. She read it all through carefully.

The journey by boat took less than a week with a fair wind. Spring is the best time.

With a fair wind. She supposed that meant Aidan's boat had a sail, and that's why he'd needed a fair wind.

How much longer would a rowing boat take?

And this wasn't springtime; it was January.

Long dark nights.

Short cold days.

Fog. Snowstorms. Gale-force winds.

Bonnie clattered noisily up the staircase.

It worked. Ish was awake by the time she got up to his bedroom.

He stretched out his arms. 'How long I sleep?'

'Hours and hours! It's dark. Dinner time.'

Ish nodded. 'Is very good soft bed. Hungry now.'

'Me too. Get up and we'll open one of those tins for supper.'

'How's Granda?'

Bonnie sighed. 'He's not well. His breathing sounds horrible. Painful.'

'He is old man,' Ish said. 'Is hard, living in cold wet places. Better in sunshine. Warm. Sitting under the lemon trees.'

Down in the little kitchen, Bonnie stabbed a can open with a knife.

She sniffed at the contents. 'I think it's a kind of bean. It might taste better heated up.' She tipped the contents into the cooking pot and put it on the stove.

Ish got out three bowls and spoons and put them on the table. He did everything very slowly, as if he were thinking about something else.

'I do not do this for a long, long time. Back home. Lay table. My mother cook supper . . .'

For a moment she imagined Ish in another country, far away from here. Somewhere warm, a soft breeze lifting a net curtain at a window, dazzling sun outside and the smell of lemons; Ish laying bowls on a wooden table and his mother stirring a pan at a stove in a small dark kitchen . . .

She nodded, to show Ish she understood how much he missed his home, how sorry she was.

The beans were delicious, they agreed. They ate half the packet of oatcakes too.

Bonnie carried a bowl up to Granda and set it on the table.

He opened his eyes a fraction. 'Not hungry, Bonnie. I think I'll try sleeping on a proper bed. You can help me up the stairs.'

'Your hands are warmer, Granda. That's good.'

She helped him take off his coat and shoes and settle down. She tucked him in.

'It's like I'm your mam. Perhaps I should tell you a bedtime story, Granda!'

His face creased in a smile. 'Another night, mebbe.'

Downstairs, Bonnie and Ish sat on the soft red seats in the living room and Bonnie showed him the sea maps and the compass she'd found.

Ish brightened up. 'This is good. We follow chart and find right land.'

'I don't understand how. It's not like there are signposts in the sea, or anything to show the way. It's empty grey water in every direction.'

'You have to see different. It's like road map of ocean. Numbers are how deep, and direction of currents, circles for rocks and marks where wrecked boats and where lights and buoys.'

'But that was then. There won't be lights and buoys now.'

'How you know? You never been in boat even.'

Ish turned away from her, and laid the compass on the map, and moved it around as if he was working something out.

She picked out a book to read instead. She looked at the one about hens, but that made her sad, thinking of Fritha left behind. She opened the book about boats and found a picture of an old-fashioned coble with a mast and sail.

She showed Ish. 'Perhaps we could make some kind of sail, to help our boat go faster with the wind.'

'Our boat?'

Bonnie sighed. 'Your boat.'

'How make a sail?'

'With a sheet from the bed. Would that be strong enough?'

'No. And how make a mast? Is impossible.'

Ish put the compass back on the table. He folded the charts and went down to the kitchen.

Bonnie refused to be defeated. There must be a way. She studied the pictures in the book but it didn't help. These boats had been properly designed to have a mast that fitted in the front of the boat, and the sails were made of a thick canvas. Sailcloth, not thin cotton sheet.

Ish reappeared, carrying a lamp and three mugs of tea balanced on a wooden tray. 'Here,' he said. 'Sorry about I cross.'

Bonnie closed the boat book. 'Thank you.'

Ish took a mug of tea upstairs to Granda.

Ish still couldn't settle. He moved from one bench seat to another, kept going to the window, tapped and jiggled his foot when he sat down. He was all on edge.

When she was like that, Granda used to tell her stories.

'Shall I tell you an old story about this island?' she said.

Ish nodded. He perched on one of the seats, head in his hands.

Bonnie curled up on the seat opposite him. She slurped the last dregs of tea.

'Once upon a time,' she began, 'long ago, there was a holy man.

'People said he could do miracles. He could talk to the birds and the seals and understand their language.'

'How do you know?' Ish asked. But he was settling himself down to listen to the story; he couldn't help himself. That was the power of stories. They drew you in and made you want to know what happened next.

'Granda told me. And his granda told him. Back and back through time.'

Ish nodded.

'Anyway, the holy man hated being cooped up inside and he didn't like being bossed about by the other holy men. He wanted to be free to think his own thoughts and to look at the sky and wonder at the amazing world. So he came to this island and lived here where no one could bother him or make him do boring stuff. When he needed fresh water a well sprang up, because he could do miracles. And he grew crops like barley and vegetables for dinner, and I expect he ate fish.'

Ish was lying on the couch now with his eyes closed. Was he still listening?

'How do we know which fish we can catch to eat?' Bonnie asked.

Ish opened an eye. 'What do you mean?'

'After the poisoning of the oceans. But some deepwater species are OK now. You don't get sick.'

'I don't know. Go back to your story. What happened to your holy man?'

In the story Granda had told Bonnie, the man eventually died, and when fierce marauding raiders were on the way to attack the island his old friends came and took his body in a coffin, by boat and then by horse and cart, to an important holy building on the mainland and buried him inside. But that seemed all wrong to Bonnie.

She made up her own ending for Ish.

'The holy man was happy, living a simple life of

growing and catching food and talking to the birds. Two crows became his special friends. He wrote stories and sang songs and drew beautiful pictures and he was happy. He wasn't ever really lonely because the people in his stories felt like family, and he was friends with the birds and creatures.'

'Even the fish?'

Bonnie smiled. 'OK, I guess he didn't eat fish after all. Anyway, he lived here until he died and he was buried here under a pile of stones.'

Ish shivered. 'Not under stones.'

'But he was already dead—' Bonnie stopped mid-sentence. She'd remembered Ish's drawings.

She took a deep breath. 'OK, so, this is what happened. When the man was very, very old and very tired, he just lay down on the cliffs one sunny spring day under the wide, blue, open sky, with the skylarks singing above him, and he died peacefully in his sleep. And the wind blew, and the seabirds called, and it was beautiful. And the world carried on.'

Ish nodded. 'Sky burial,' he said.

They were both quiet for ages.

'What you think happens when someone dies?' Ish asked.

'I don't know. It's all a mystery. How can someone simply not be there any more?' Bonnie frowned. 'Maybe they just become part of the air, the elements which everything came from in the first place. Stardust.'

Ish was silent. He swallowed hard.

Bonnie was almost too scared to ask. 'Have you . . . Did you . . . ? Did someone in your family die?'

His voice when it came was so quiet she could hardly hear. 'My mother my father my baby brother my grandmother.'

He bowed his head. The sadness went so deep he couldn't cry.

Bonnie sat quietly. There was nothing she could say.

Maybe some day Ish would want to tell her more about his family and what had happened. Maybe he'd tell her happy memories too, from before the war. But not yet; probably not for a long, long time.

Sometimes all we can do, Granda had told her, is be a witness to someone else's suffering. And even that can seem unbearable. But we must do it. Stay there. Hear and see it.

The lamp flickered and sent shadows darting around the small room. Outside, the cold darkness pressed against the lighthouse windows, and the sea swept over the rocks.

The sea never stopped. Wave after wave after wave, day and night, from since time began until time ended.

Granda's words came to her again. *Create a better world.*

That was what they had to do now.

Storm

Bonnie woke in the night, her heart thudding. What had she heard?

The wind must have woken her. It howled and screeched and whistled and most terrifying of all, made deep, booming echoes. Massive waves hurled themselves at the rocks, and each time they broke over the island, everything in the lighthouse shuddered.

She needed the loo.

She went down the spiral staircase carefully in the dark, holding on tight to the rail. *It's quite safe*, she told herself as everything shook with another gust of wind. *This building has been here for hundreds of years.* She paused when she got to the room below. The bedclothes on

Ish's bed had been kicked back, and his bed was empty.

She carried on down.

Granda was lying on his back, his head propped on two cushions. His breath came in noisy, rattling gasps.

'Granda?' she whispered. 'You alright?'

No answer. He was sound asleep. He looked so thin and small and flat, somehow, lying under the covers. A shell of the man he'd once been.

She carried on down, through the sitting room, the kitchen: there was no sign of Ish here, either. Perhaps he too had been woken by the storm and had gone up to the top, to look out of the glass dome. She stepped down into the entrance hall and opened the door to the loo. She should have fetched a pail of water to flush it. She'd do that in the morning when it was light.

She turned to go up the stairs again.

The coat hook was empty. Mam's sheepskin coat was gone. She checked again in case it had fallen onto the floor. Had she left it somewhere else? Or perhaps Ish had borrowed it.

A terrible thought flashed into her mind. Ish had taken the coat and the boat, abandoned her and Granda . . .

Surely he wouldn't do such a thing, not after all she'd

done for him. In any case, it would be impossible in a wild storm like this, in pitch dark.

She opened the door a crack, and the wind rushed in and snatched it back on its hinges. 'Ish?' she yelled out into the night.

He was running down the path towards the jetty, a slight figure in a too-big coat. She called out again but there was no way he'd ever hear.

She raced after him. The wind was freezing, drenched with sea spray. She slithered and slipped on the wet ground. She was soaked to the skin and shivering. This was madness.

And then she realized what Ish was doing.

'NO! NO! NO!' Bonnie yelled.

The wind and the waves were too strong for the rope to hold the boat fast.

The knot had come undone, or the rope had broken under the strain, and their boat—Ish's boat—was in danger of being smashed into pieces by the waves. He was trying to save the boat.

She ran down onto the jetty. She tried to pull Ish back. 'NO! It's too dangerous. You'll get yourself drowned!'

Ish pushed her away. He jumped down onto the thin strip of beach. He was already wading into the waves after the boat.

Bonnie jumped too. She waded into the water, grabbed the hem of Mam's coat to keep Ish steady while he flailed around trying to catch hold of the rope.

They were too late. The boat had broken free, was drifting, the two oars floating away, swept out by the current.

Ish shouted words she didn't understand. He cried out, a sound so full of anger and sorrow and despair it filled Bonnie with terror.

Another massive wave smashed onto the beach and knocked both Ish and Bonnie off their feet. There was the sound of splintering wood.

She scrabbled up, swallowed a mouthful of salt water, almost slipped again, found her balance just in time before the next wave swept in.

She grabbed for Ish's hand.

As she did so, she saw that the next terrible, powerful wave was lifting the boat. It hurled it as if it were no heavier than a pebble back onto the shore. The sea spat the boat out, like Jonah and the whale.

Together, Bonnie and Ish dragged themselves out of the water, up onto the sand, and held on tight to the battered boat as the wave sucked back with a roar.

Together, they lifted the boat and heaved it over, to drain the seawater out.

Together, with another huge effort of will, they managed to push and shove and haul the heavy boat right up the beach, out of the reach of the sea.

Bonnie had no strength left. She keeled over next to the boat.

Ish collapsed beside her in a sodden heap. 'I thought we'd never get it back. Thought it was all over.' He began to weep.

And now he'd started, he could not stop.

Alone

The gale kept blowing. Ish and Granda both stayed in bed all the next day. Bonnie took them food and drink but neither ate a thing.

'You must eat, Granda,' Bonnie said. 'You need to keep your strength up.'

But Granda said he was too tired, and not hungry, and although he sipped at the hot tea she brought him, he mostly slept.

His breathing was worse. She wished she had medicine to give him—honey, or herbs, or something to ease the pain in his chest. She wished the storm would stop: sunshine and blue skies would help Granda feel better, she was sure.

Ish had descended into a deep black gloom and nothing Bonnie said or did made the slightest difference. He blamed himself for not bringing the boat up onto the land as he had always done before. How stupid, to leave it tied up. He knew how a calm sea changes in minutes, how the weather can change from sea fret to stormforce winds, how everything changes all the time out on the ocean. What had possessed him? How had he forgotten everything he had ever learned?

Was it her fault? Bonnie wanted to know. Was it the knot she tied that had come undone?

'Of course not. It my fault. I am responsible. I know not to leave a boat tied in storm.'

'But it was all OK in the end,' Bonnie said. 'That's all that matters. We saved the boat. It's only a bit bashed about. We can make new oars. It's going to be alright, Ish.'

'Please eat something,' Bonnie begged him at dinnertime.

'We must ration food,' Ish said. 'How long it last?'

'We can catch fish,' Bonnie said.

Ish huffed.

'And we can collect driftwood, and make two new oars.'

She kept on. 'There must be other people crossing the ocean. I've seen boats in the distance before. Maybe a passing boat will pick us up and help us get to a safe place.'

'You really think that possible? You stupid.' Ish turned his face to the wall.

'At least I'm not just sleeping all the time.'

Bonnie left him to it.

She climbed up to the top of the lighthouse, up the ladder and out onto the wooden platform under the glass dome.

She stared out into the darkness. Ships would have lights of some kind. But there was not a single light out there. She must be able to see for miles now the sea fret had lifted. There was nothing. No one.

Granda was really sick.

Ish had given up hope. Perhaps it was not surprising, after everything that had happened to him. She thought of the way he had sobbed last night, how impossible it had been to offer him comfort.

Maybe he was right and she was stupid. The massive cargo ship she'd seen that day from the beach . . . how could a ship like that possibly spot a tiny rowing boat with three people on it, bobbing on the waves? Just the

wake from such a huge ship would capsize and drown
them.

They'd done so well to get here.

So now to be stuck—it seemed especially cruel.

She had never felt so utterly alone.

Dandelion

The storm lasted seven days and nights, and for most of that time Ish kept to himself.

Granda was getting weaker each day. Bonnie sat with him, and held his hand. She told him she loved him; she needed him to get better. She tried to feed him porridge, and beans, but he ate little more than a sparrow. In the evenings, she read poems to him, and stroked his head, and sang to him the songs he'd once sung to her.

'My pearl beyond price,' Granda whispered. 'My sweet delight.'

Bonnie knew how important it was to get up every morning, eat food, get exercise, make plans. Every morning, after she'd made breakfast of porridge with oats and water, she scoured the island beach for driftwood and sea coal. She brought it back to the lighthouse to dry out. She studied the boat book to learn about currents and sailing and to help her understand the charts.

She spread out the roll of paper and left the tin of pencils by Ish's bed. The paper and pencils were the only things they'd managed to hold onto through everything that had happened. Maybe Ish would start drawing again, and that would help him feel better. He had said hardly a word for seven days.

On the eighth morning, the wind dropped. The sea stayed rough for another two days, and then that calmed too. The sky cleared and there was the first beautiful golden sunrise she'd seen in ages.

Bonnie took her breakfast to eat outside in the sheltered walled garden. She lifted her face to feel the first sensation of warmth. Yes, spring would come, and fair weather, and soon they could go on with their journey.

She leant back against the wall. She shifted position to get more comfortable against the rough surface and as she did so she saw something yellow on the stone—not lichen as she first thought, but a weathered drawing of a flower.

A yellow dandelion flower.

Bonnie stared at it.

The drawing nudged something at the back of her mind.

She studied it more carefully. It was small, the size of an actual dandelion flower. But the style was familiar. She ran her finger over the flaking golden paint, the inked outline . . . Yes! It was like a tiny version of the flower in the hands of the girl in the massive mural in the house in the woods.

The same person who had drawn the mural had surely done this, too.

What did it mean?

She puzzled over it for ages while she finished her porridge.

It meant the person had travelled here.

And that meant they must have had a boat.

And if the person who had painted the mural had been Aidan . . . Then he had been here, too.

Later, when she ran down to the beach with the buckets to collect driftwood and sea coal washed up by the high tide, she thought again about the stacks of food, the bedding, Ish's notion that the house of light was prepared ready for someone.

She thought about that other house, back in the dark

woods. The mural, but also the runaway man and his scribble in yellow pencil.

It was all connected, she was sure of it.

She jumped down from the jetty onto the damp sand. The seven-day storm had washed up all kinds of stuff each high tide. This morning there was a ridge of healthy seaweed, freshly churned up from deep water. She filled a bucket with the brown fleshy leaves. Forest kelp. She could dry it, and use it to flavour soups. It would help eke out the tins. She found the red leaves of dulse lower down, still attached to rocks, and picked some of that too. She only took enough for a few meals. It was important never to take too much from the plant so it could stay alive. She searched for razor clams but the tide was still too high. She picked up lumps of sea coal. Further along the beach she discovered an old fence post made of larch. Surely that could be turned into an oar. She dragged it up to the top of the beach to dry out.

She walked back up the path to the lighthouse.

She found Ish sitting on the doorstep, eyes closed, his face held up to the sun. He looked peaceful; more relaxed than she had ever seen him.

'Look! My morning haul.' She plonked the buckets down on the path. She explained about drying seaweed, and how good it is for you, full of nutrients. She didn't say anything about the last nine days. Better not to.

'I found something, too,' he said.

'What?'

'You have to come and see. Follow me.'

She stopped when they got to Granda's room.

'Are you awake?' she asked him. 'The sun's out this morning. It's *almost* warm. We should get you out into the garden for some fresh air, Granda. It will give you an appetite.'

'Mebbe,' he said. 'You're a good lass.' He nodded at Ish. 'And you too, son—not so bad.'

Ish looked confused. 'Is good or bad?' he asked Bonnie.

'Good: it means he likes you.'

Granda coughed feebly. Bonnie propped him up more with an extra pillow. 'There,' she said. 'That's better.'

Ish was waiting, impatient to show her what he'd discovered.

'I'll be back in a minute, Granda.' She followed Ish up the rest of the spiral staircase.

They got to the ladder, and clambered out onto the platform.

'OH!' Bonnie gasped. A small brass telescope was mounted on a wooden tripod, pointing out to sea.

She rushed over to look through. 'Where was it? How did you find it?'

'I find key in one of the drawers downstairs, and it fits keyhole in the cupboard under the ladder, and this is inside, folded.'

For a moment, everything swayed out of focus. She twisted the telescope, and reeled back as everything rushed closer, larger, in focus. She could see the near islands in detail: rocks, birds, the pattern of lichens above the tideline. She swivelled it round again. The line of the coast came into distant view. Pale sand, darker hills behind with snow on the high moorland.

'Can they see us, now it's clear?'

'No. Many many miles. It has powerful lens. Makes very long distance look small.'

Bonnie swivelled around again. A massive seagull blocked the view for a second, and then it soared away and there was nothing but sea, blue in the sunshine under a clear sky.

'We can keep watch,' she said.

'We can study ships that pass near.' Ish took a turn to look through the telescope.

'We'll need to wait for Granda to get better, in any case. He's too weak to travel.'

They were both quiet for a bit.

Would he get better? Bonnie wondered. *What if he didn't?*

'How many food tins are left?' Ish asked.

'Loads, more than thirty. That's a month's worth of dinner, especially if we can catch fish and forage from the shore. In any case, we shouldn't be in a rush. The weather will be better, the longer we can hold out.'

All that day, Bonnie kept climbing up to the top to look through the telescope.

The sunlight played tricks on distances. Sometimes it seemed to bring the mainland closer.

Had they been right to leave?

Deep down she knew there was no future for her back on the mainland. No real freedom or happiness. The place she'd called home had changed forever. The only thing to do was to find a way to go on with their journey, to cross the sea to the safe place Aidan wrote about, where she might find news of Mam.

Ish had been studying the navigation charts. He showed her how the shipping channels were marked, and the routes between the countries in the south-east and the free north. 'These will be friendly ships,' he told her. 'Travelling between free countries where there is no war, and people are not obsessed with borders and laws about who can live where.' He'd watch with the telescope tonight, to see if he could spot them, work out the times and days they travelled.

Bonnie watched the sea all afternoon, and saw not a single ship.

At dusk, when she turned the telescope back towards the mainland coast, she glimpsed the low grey shape of the patrol boat.

'Ish?' she called down. 'The border patrol boat is going along the coast right now. Check the time.'

How? There were no clocks.

Dusk she wrote down later on a page in the notepad downstairs. *Travelling slowly along coast, north. One border patrol boat.* She added the words, *Day* 1. In reality, this was island day . . . she tried to count . . . day ten? Eleven?

She flipped back through the notepad. She stopped again at the pages with the numbers. They were scribbled in black ink, not pencil.

Drawing ink.

Like the dandelion flower.

Like the drawings in the letters from *A* to Mam.

It was Aidan who had painted the girl, and the dandelion flower. She was sure of it. He'd stopped off here at the island when he made his journey across the sea. And maybe others had done that too. Maybe the runaway man would make his way here. And the girl on the headland who had watched them, too.

Maybe her own mam had slept in one of the beds in the house of light, her heart full of fear and worry and excitement, just like Bonnie.

Notes

Bonnie and Ish sat together on the red couch in the sitting room. Granda was sleeping upstairs. He'd slept most of the day. It was already beginning to get dark.

Bonnie lit the lamp with the flint striker and brought it over to the table. She peered over Ish's shoulder at the open notebook.

'So, can you see any pattern?'

'Border patrol boat goes up and down the mainland coast, just as begins to get dark or early morning. It not come out to sea at all.'

'That's good,' Bonnie said.

'One cargo ship travel from north to south in the daytime. Day 3, see?'

'And maybe the lights you saw were from the same ship going north, three days later, but at night-time,' Bonnie said.

Ish spread out the sea chart on the table and traced his finger along the shipping channel marked with dotted lines. 'Is going up and back this way, I think yes.'

'There's only one ship a week, really. That we can see from here, anyway. There might be others further away, I guess.'

'Is enough,' Ish said. 'So, listen. This is my idea.'

Bonnie leant back against the wall of the house of light. The solid stone felt strong, almost warm, holding her safe.

'We row north-north-east, towards the shipping channel. We try to time it so we see the cargo ship go north ahead of us. We wait. We follow ship's wake; it take us direction to safe harbour on northland coast. We stay back, so we don't capsize in ship's wake. Just follow the white line ahead. We see that even in dark. If ship go at night.'

Bonnie swallowed. It had been terrifying to be in the tiny boat in a mist. Imagine it in the dark! All day and all night, for how many days and nights? They would be exhausted. Like Ish had been, when he first arrived at the beach . . . If they didn't capsize, or get swamped by a passing whale, or get carried away by the current . . . or . . . freeze to death under the glittering stars.

She imagined the white line of the wake fading and disintegrating in the dark sea. They'd never keep up.

'I suppose we can set the compass, so we row in the right direction, even after the ship has gone.'

Ish nodded. 'Of course. Three days won't be enough to get to land. We must therefore keep out of way of ship coming the other way on its return journey.'

She shuddered. 'Aidan's letter said it took a week, with a fair wind . . . How much faster is a sailing boat than a little rowing boat?'

'Some, I not sure how many. I teach you to row; practise, so we can take turns, yes?'

Bonnie nodded.

'We take turns to row, we sleep in turns, we navigate in turns. Is only way now, Bonnie. Or you stay here forever. Is your choice.'

'You know I want to come with you. Just not yet. I can't leave Granda.'

'Yes. I understand.'

Bonnie's heart ached. 'He's much too ill to come any further.'

Granda

'Tell me about the day Mam left,' Bonnie said.

Granda was dozing in a chair in the February sunshine. It was just about warm enough with a blanket wrapped around him, out of the shelter of the wind in the walled garden. 'I want to be outside,' he'd told Bonnie when she went to see him at breakfast time. 'I want to see the sky and smell the air and feel the sunlight on my face.' So Bonnie and Ish had helped him all the way down the spiral stairs. It had taken all Granda's breath.

He opened his eyes.

Bonnie was startled by the intensity of his gaze. His eyes seemed paler blue, and full of light. It was if he were looking at her but also beyond her, *through* her, almost, to something she couldn't see.

Bonnie pulled the blanket closer around him, and tucked his hands inside. He wasn't going to get better; she understood that now. He was too frail and thin and ill and worn out. But his eyes! Piercing and brilliant, almost fierce.

She held up the cup for him. Water was all he wanted. He hadn't eaten for several days.

He held one hand against his chest as he coughed and coughed. The wracked sound made Bonnie ache inside.

'Do you remember that day, Granda?' she asked again. 'When Mam left?'

'Not really. It's such a long time ago. I imagine it was an ordinary day. Maybe we argued again about her going away.' Granda's voice rasped, as if his throat was too dry. He had to keep taking breaths just to get the words out.

'I expect she played with you, and made your food, and put you down for a nap in the afternoon. She must have been packing. Preparing the boat. I didn't know about that.'

Bonnie waited for him to catch his breath. 'What did she play with me?'

Granda smiled weakly. 'Oh, the usual. Horsey rides with you on her back. Hide-and-seek, mebbe. *Where's*

Bonnie gone? she'd call out, pretending she couldn't see you. You liked that. You laughed and laughed.'

He stopped to sip more water. 'Sometimes she'd sing, and although you had only just started to walk, you'd jiggle, both feet on the ground, as if you were dancing.'

'What songs?'

'All the old ones. The same ones I taught you. The nursery rhymes, and one about a farm. We'd make the animal noises. One about bluebells.'

'And the Skye boat song?'

Granda nodded.

'My Bonnie lies over the ocean.'

Granda didn't speak.

They were sad songs, about loss and separation.

Granda started to sing in his wavering voice, too quietly for Bonnie to hear the words. She knelt close to him to try to hear. Something about *light, love. 'Travelling through this world* . . .' He stopped to cough. He reached out for Bonnie's hand. 'They called these the Pilgrim Islands. The Wanderers' Isles.'

'Who did?'

'Folk back in the days of the civilized world. A thousand years ago. In those days, you welcomed a stranger at your door. Gave them food and shelter.'

Bonnie nodded. She'd heard Granda say this many times.

'Not like the dark ages we are living through now.

'But the good times will return,' Granda whispered. 'You, Bonnie, helping the stranger boy: you're already making the world a better place. You two together. Look after each other.'

Bonnie couldn't speak. Her throat was too tight.

'You'll be fine, Bonnie, when I'm gone. It won't be long now. You and the boy, you must get ready, head out to sea. There will be others join you, travelling the old route. Like those who went before.'

Bonnie swallowed hard. 'Like Mam, and Aidan.'

Granda nodded. 'Others, too. People like you, wanting to create a better life, or seeking a safe home, like the boy.'

A flock of small birds flew over the garden. Granda watched them settle on the dried seed heads next to the wall.

'Goldfinch,' he said. 'A charm of goldfinches. A long way from home.'

'I saw a cormorant yesterday down on the rocks,' Bonnie said, 'with its wings stretched out. You told me about them, how they have to do that to dry their feathers.'

'Where's the boy?'

'Ish? He's making another oar, so we have a spare one. I'd better go and help. You OK out here by yourself a little while?'

Granda nodded. He closed his eyes again. 'I'm grand. The light is astonishing.'

She found Ish working at the top of the beach. The tide was low. Small birds—sanderlings and dunlin—ran in and out of the foam at the edge of the water, sieving for shrimps with their flat bills. The birds here took little notice of her or Ish. They had no fear. Perhaps they had never met people before. Or only kind ones.

'The boat looks good,' Bonnie said.

Ish nodded. He held the dried-out larch pole steady between his knees while he shaved the edges at one end to form a kind of paddle shape. He'd drawn the design on paper, copying the pictures in the boat book. He was using a kitchen knife to carve the wood.

'People spend years learning how to build a boat and shape an oar,' Bonnie said. 'You're doing a grand job.'

'Is still not right,' Ish said. 'Need a wider, flatter piece of wood, really.' He held out his hands. 'But this is all we have.'

'Granda's very weak,' Bonnie said. Her eyes welled up.

'Go back to him,' Ish said. 'He needs you. I am fine working like this.'

Bonnie sat down. 'In a minute.'

'Is too hard, yes?'

She nodded. She rested her head on her knees and let the tears come.

It was so quiet and peaceful here, with the birds and the steady sound of Ish chipping away at the wood. The sun was warm, even the wind coming off the sea had lost its harsh edge.

An early spring, a fair wind.

She walked slowly back up the slope to the house.

Bonnie knew, the moment she stepped through the gateway into the walled garden.

Granda was slumped in the chair, head lolled back against the wall, his eyes closed.

She didn't run. Everything went into slow motion, as if she was watching herself take the last steps towards him, touch his hand, his cheek.

She rested her hand on his chest to feel for a heartbeat; she held his wrist for a pulse, but there was none.

'Goodbye, Granda,' she whispered, even though he could no longer hear her. 'Thank you.'

She sat with him for a while. There was nothing to be afraid of. This was Granda's body, like a shell, but real Granda was no longer there. He was free as a bird; he was part of the air and the light and the beautiful world, and he was also part of her, forever.

'Ish?' she called.

She needed him. She called again, louder, and he came running.

Together, later, they carried Granda through the gate, across the top of the island, to the far edge where the white waves broke over the rocks, where the wind blew, where the seabirds soared and cried. They laid his body on the quiet earth. They hardly said a word. Bonnie knew what to do by a kind of instinct, by listening to her own heart, and Ish helped her, stayed at her side, put his hand on her back to say he knew, and he understood, and he was her friend.

25

A Fair Wind

Life simply carries on, even when someone you love dies. That was the strange truth Bonnie discovered. She carried on doing her usual daily things—she got up, made porridge, worked with Ish on the boat, practised rowing in the shelter of the little harbour, studied the sea charts with him, kept watch through the telescope up in the dome, slept. It seemed to help, just to do practical ordinary things.

Outside, the world seemed vivid and sharply focused and breathtakingly beautiful, as if she suddenly saw the preciousness of life around her. The birds that foraged on the beach or rested on the rocks and everywhere around the island soared in the clear sky seemed miraculous to her. She noticed the subtle changes of light on the water. Each sunrise and sunset was astonishing.

Ish was beginning to feel almost like family.

He of all people could understand the sorrow she carried inside her. He'd lost everything too.

'We're both refugees now,' Bonnie said. 'We've left our old worlds behind. But we have each other.'

They were down on the little beach. The tide was high.

Bonnie turned to face the sea. 'The wind has changed direction.'

Ish nodded. 'Is from the south-west.'

'*A fair wind.* Like in Aidan's letter.'

'Time to go, soon. The boat is ready.'

Bonnie picked up a flat white pebble from the beach. She had collected a pile of them—white, cream, pale grey.

'What are they for?' Ish asked.

'I want to make something for Granda. I'm going to draw on the stones, and write words. In his memory.'

'A bit like a gravestone.'

'Sort of. But I want it to be bright and colourful. You can help if you want.'

They heaped the pebbles into the canvas bag Bonnie

had brought down to the beach, and she carried them back up the slope. The stones clinked against each other in rhythm with her steps. She tipped them out again on the garden path and arranged them according to size.

Ish went inside.

He came back with the little box of paints, and a fine paint brush, and a roll of paper.

'You found the paints! I knew you'd like them.'

He unrolled the paper and showed her his picture of a house in a garden, in bright oil colours.

Bonnie studied closely the detail of the plants in the garden, the pattern of light and shade, the people sitting around a table. 'It's your family. Your home.'

He nodded.

'It's beautiful. Will the colours work on stones?'

'Yes.'

Bonnie tried to paint a flower shape with the yellow, but the paint blobbed and smudged.

'Have another go, much less paint. Draw an outline first?' Ish delved into his pocket. 'Here.'

Bonnie turned the pen over in her hand. It felt smooth and cool. She thought of the dandelion drawing on the wall.

'It was in one of those drawers upstairs in the sitting room cabinet.'

Bonnie nodded. 'I know. I saw it, on the very first day here.'

'It's a good one. Old fashioned. You can refill the ink.'

The nib felt scratchy but it drew a fine black line. She drew a bird, a goldfinch. She coloured it in carefully with paint.

All afternoon, they worked outside, drawing on the stones with ink, colouring them, leaving them in the air to dry. Bonnie made a flock of goldfinches, one at a time, a single cormorant, a curlew, a flight of black-and-white oystercatchers, a black hen. She drew a dandelion, like the one on the wall. Ish painted a tiny rowing boat, a house, a tree, a candle.

Bonnie thought about the words she wanted to write.

For my beloved Granda

from Bonnie

Love

Freedom

Justice

Peace

Beauty.

'We could put the pebbles in the ruined chapel,' Ish said. 'They'd be out of the wind and rain there.'

Bonnie shook her head. 'I want them high up, in the air and light and close to the sky.'

They walked together across the top of the island to the highest point. The wind blew strong and fresh, bringing the smell of the salt sea. Grey-and-white kittiwakes called from the cliff edges below. Bonnie knelt on the thin grass and arranged the painted pebbles in a spiral shape, starting with the smallest, winding round to the biggest, with the word-pebbles right at the heart.

'It's beautiful,' Ish said.

Bonnie stood up. 'Now we sing something.'

'OK, you start.'

Bonnie sang the *Skye Boat Song*, and *My Bonnie*, and Ish joined in with the bits he knew, and then he sang his own song, in his own language.

Shalom shalom may peace be with you . . .

Bonnie tried to remember a poem that Granda had read her. It was an ancient blessing. She could only remember the beginning, but that was good enough. She said the words aloud.

Deep peace of the running wave to you
Deep peace of the flowing air to you

Deep peace of the quiet earth to you
Deep peace of the shining stars to you.

Ish went back to the house, but Bonnie stayed there a long time, breathing in the salt air and letting the deep peace come gently into her heart.

So, it was done. Her memorial for Granda would stay there, and maybe other people would find it one day, and wonder about his story and imagine the people who had painted the stones.

She didn't want to see again the place where they had laid his body, so she walked straight back across the top of the island. All the snow had long gone. The grass was greening up, beginning to grow again. Even the bird cries had a different note, as if they too knew that winter was almost over.

Ish was in the sitting room, crouched over a white sheet spread on the floor.

'What's that?'

'It's going to be a white flag. We can wave it when we see any ships so they spot us. And white means peace.' He carried on sewing down one edge. 'This is so we can put a stick like a flagpole.' He smiled at her.

'It's almost big enough for a sail,' Bonnie said.

'It will help us check wind direction, maybe.'

Bonnie sat down on one of the soft couches under the window. She watched the fine, fair-weather clouds scudding on the south-westerly wind.

'Granda said something about other people joining us on the route,' she said.

Ish sewed more big running stitches.

'I've thought about what he meant. I reckon this is a secret place people meet, before they make the journey together across the sea. People escaping their old life. And that's why everything is ready, prepared for guests.'

Ish carried on sewing his big stitches up the side of the long edge of the sheet.

'I reckon Aidan came here, all that time ago, and he did that drawing on the garden wall. While he waited for the right wind.'

Ish tied a knot and bit off the end of the thread.

'You've seen it? The dandelion flower, like a small version of the mural at the house in the woods.'

Ish nodded.

'So maybe we should wait for the next people to come. Travel with them. It might be safer to be in a group.'

'What if no one come? Or the wrong people? Bad people.'

Bonnie hesitated. Should she mention the runaway man? That he might make his way here? It was only her guess . . . or maybe a hope . . .

Ish kept talking. 'We have charts, compass. We know when the big trade ship travels north along the channel on map. We row out and wait for the big ship to pass. We keep distance. But we follow the white water of the wake, behind. Is good plan.'

Bonnie supposed so. It was their only plan, really. Risky. Terrifying. Bold.

Ish stopped sewing and looked directly at her. 'We should go while the wind is with us.'

26

Goodbye

Should they go? Was Ish right?

Bonnie could not sleep.

How would they ever make the journey safely across the sea?

But there was no way she was going back to her old world. There was nothing for her there.

And she couldn't stay here on the island forever. She wasn't the holy man from the old tale. She had her whole life ahead of her.

She felt sure that somewhere out there, Mam was waiting for her.

Her future was waiting to unfold.

She slipped out of bed and wrapped the blanket

around her. Clear nights meant frost. She climbed up the stairs and the ladder, out onto the wooden platform under the glass dome.

Outside, it was pitch dark. She rotated the telescope, studied the sea in every direction. No light anywhere.

She angled the telescope to look up, and there, suddenly, the night sky was revealed in all its glory, glittering with hard points of light from stars that had existed thousands of years ago and might not even be there any more. The universe was so vast, and each person on this one planet was so small, and lived for so short a spell of time—the flight of a sparrow—and yet each was infinitely precious.

That was Granda talking in her head again!

He was part of her, and he always would be, however far she travelled. He hadn't tried to stop her and Ish from leaving. He had given his blessing. *Go and create a better life.* He had come with them without a moment's hesitation.

Bonnie sat down on the wooden platform and pulled the blanket tight. She felt closer to Granda high up like this, under the canopy of stars.

She must have fallen asleep. When she woke, cold and stiff, the sky was beginning to lighten in the east. Dawn. She stayed to watch the sunrise, the gold light spreading from the first faint gleam above the horizon until it coloured the whole sky and then softened to pale pink and blue.

What would they need for a long journey? Tins of beans, a knife, water, charts, compass, the big white flag, a lantern, and lamp oil. That was about all they could carry on the boat.

She was full of excitement now. She ran down the stairs, and woke Ish.

'It's the perfect morning. Time to pack and go.'

It didn't take long to get everything ready. They stuffed the cans of food, the knife and blankets into Granda's canvas haversack.

Bonnie handed Ish Granda's thick old winter coat and scarf and gloves.

'You sure?'

'Yes. Granda would want you to have them. He doesn't need them any more.

'But maybe we should leave the blankets behind,' Bonnie said, 'for the next people.'

'You can die of cold. Take one, at least.'

'OK.'

'I copy these numbers from the notepad.' Ish showed her. 'I think maybe they are coordinates for a land map. Directions.'

Bonnie peered at the scribbled numbers. Maybe he was right. Maybe the numbers really would help them find their way to the safe wooden house with its blue painted doors and windows, the vegetable patch and the lake and the forest. It couldn't do any harm to bring them, anyway.

She locked the lighthouse door and put the key back under the stone. 'Thank you,' she said out loud, like Granda had taught her. She ran to catch up Ish.

They stowed everything best they could under the seats. Bonnie waited on the jetty while Ish climbed down into the boat and picked up the oars.

'And you're absolutely sure it's still watertight?'

'We tested it, didn't we? It's all good.'

'I'll just say one last goodbye to Granda.'

'Quick, then. We should leave on the ebbing tide.'

Bonnie ran up the sloping path, over the top of the island to the memorial. She said the words of the old blessing one last time. She told Granda she loved him, and she would always miss him, but he was in her heart forever.

The south-westerly wind dried her cheeks.

She turned away for the last time.

The boat was tugging on the mooring as if eager to be gone. Bonnie untied the rope and climbed down the steps and into the boat.

Ish picked up the oars.

Bonnie set the compass north-north-east. She pulled up the collar of Mam's coat. She settled on the wooden seat, feet tucked firmly under.

The sky was blue streaked with fine white cloud. And the air was suddenly filled with the familiar, strange voices of geese calling to each other as they began their own long migration flight.

'Look!' Bonnie pointed skywards. 'The pink-footed geese are coming with us! They're showing us the way!'

27

At Sea

The geese had disappeared into the pale sky ahead, flying much faster than Bonnie and Ish could row. The wind blew fair and steady; the sky cleared to blue, the waves were less choppy now they'd cleared the last of the little islands. To begin with, Ish rowed, and Bonnie sang a rhythm, and then they swapped places (scary, it made the boat rock) and Bonnie took her first turn of rowing at sea. They swapped back when her hands began to hurt. This time, she worked out how to shift seats without making the boat rock so violently: be swift, crouch down, keep her centre of gravity low in the boat.

Bonnie held her sore palms against the softness of her sheepskin coat.

'Your skin will toughen up,' Ish told her. 'But the blisters hurt at first.'

Salt water made them sting. But Bonnie knew the salt helped them stay clean, too.

Now the geese had gone, everything seemed extra quiet. There was just the slap of water against the boat, the creak of the oars. The wind ruffled the cotton flag where it lay in the bottom of the boat.

Ish and Bonnie stopped talking.

The hours passed, and nothing changed but the angle of sunlight on the water.

Ish rowed, Bonnie held the compass to keep them on course. Around them, there was nothing but sea, sea, sea all the way to the horizon. There were no boats in any direction. It was unnerving to be the only visible living things for miles and miles. If they capsized the boat no one would see, no one would come to help. They were entirely alone.

Bonnie thought about life under the sea: fish, and plankton, and crabs and lobsters and jellyfish and octopus and squid and thousands and millions of shellfish crawling over the seabed. It made her feel less lonely, to think of all that life going on beneath the surface. The sea here was relatively shallow, Granda had taught her. Once upon a time, many thousands of years ago, it had been dry land, and animals had roamed freely across it. People, too. Sea levels rose and fell over centuries. The terrible wars and industrial waste and pollution had changed the climate, melted the polar ice, drowned islands and made sea levels rise. Only recently had life started to return to the oceans. Whales, seals, dolphins: maybe she and Ish would actually see some. *But not too close up,* she hoped. A whale could capsize a small boat.

They were both exhausted, but they made themselves carry on, taking turns to row and to navigate. When they both felt ravenously hungry, they ate oatcakes and beans spooned from a can. They sipped from the bottle of water, to make sure it would last the journey.

It was hard to tell how much time had passed: the only clue came as the light began to fade.

'Should I light the lantern?' Bonnie finally asked. 'Or is it best to wait till we see lights from another boat?'

'Yes, wait,' Ish said. 'Save fuel.' He rested the oars, and the boat rocked and moved gently, the wind and waves carrying it forward.

It's just darkness, Bonnie told herself. *No need to be*

scared. Even so, she was glad to see the pale moon rise in the east, and the first star. Venus. The evening star, Granda called it, even though it was really a planet not a star.

As the moon rose higher, it cast a pale pathway across the water.

Something else gleamed silvery-green in the sea around the boat. She leaned over to see better.

Phosphorescence: from microscopic plankton creatures. She'd heard of that, and here it was!

'Look!' she showed Ish. 'Isn't that beautiful?'

Now the sun had gone, it was much colder. She was glad they'd brought the blanket. She tucked it around her legs. 'You can have it when it's my turn to row.'

Ish nodded. 'Our first night at sea. Is OK, yes?'

Bonnie smiled. 'At least it's calm.'

Ish rowed on.

Then it was Bonnie's turn again. They shifted seats.

Ish sat back. He pushed both his hands deep in the coat pockets. 'This very good coat. Warm. Like your granda boots.'

'I'm glad,' Bonnie said.

Ish frowned slightly. 'Is paper something in here,' he said. He pulled the paper out and peered at it.

In the pale moonlight Bonnie saw the rectangular shape.

'What is it?' she said, even though it was obvious it was an envelope. 'What does it say on the front?'

Ish held it higher, so she could see what was written on the front in the faint light of the moon.

For Bonnie. To be given to her on her 14th Birthday.

Bonnie's hands were shaking. She stopped rowing. She knew that handwriting. She'd seen it before. But it wasn't Granda's.

'Swap seats again. I'll row,' Ish said.

'Careful! Don't drop it!' Bonnie snatched it from him. Shakily, she opened the creased and faded envelope and slid out the letter inside.

She unfolded the page and smoothed it out. There was barely enough light to read all the words, but she managed it. She read it through three times without speaking. She could hardly breathe.

Ish rowed on silently. The waves slapped against the hull of the boat as they moved on. Above them, the cold stars glittered in the dark.

Dear Bonnie,

I love you more than anything. It breaks my heart to leave you behind. I know you will be loved and cherished and safe with my dad, your granda, but it still breaks my heart.

I imagine you aged 14.

I hope you're well and happy. I know your granda will have raised you with love, taught you wonderful things about the world, read you stories and sung you songs, because that is how he raised me. And so I also know that you have a strong mind and an independent spirit. You are brave and curious and kind, with a sense of fairness and justice.

(Keep reading, Bonnie, please. Try to understand. Forgive me.)

I've wanted to leave this dark land for so long, to build a new and better life in a free country which values people, and love, and music, and art. Life gets meaner here every day. There are new restrictions every week. Now the authorities want to stop people travelling. I need to go before it is too late. I had planned that we would all go, you and me and Aidan and your granda too, if I could persuade him. But the journey is too dangerous and uncertain. I cannot risk your life. Dad is right.

I have to go now so that the new baby I am expecting can have a chance of life. There is a terrible sickness, the Seven Day Death, which took our baby, Fritha, last winter, and we have no medicines to stop it. I cannot bear for this to happen a second time. Aidan has already gone ahead.

Tonight I go. I kiss you goodbye.

If I can, I will come back for you. But if you are reading this letter, it means I have not yet found a way to do that.

Maybe, one day you too will make a journey to a new life.

Whatever you decide to do, Bonnie, be happy, be yourself, be free. Live the best life you can.

Know that I will never stop loving you, and that leaving you is the hardest thing I will ever do.

Your mam,

Frances Mary Penn

Bonnie turned over the page. A map hand-drawn in ink showed a coastline, and a road, a track through a forest, and a dotted line like a path. She peered in the darkness: it was getting harder to see, but she thought there were lines, like a kind of grid, and maybe numbers. In the corner was a sketch of a dandelion seed, like a tiny parachute.

Ish watched her anxiously. 'Is OK?' he asked, when finally she folded the page back into the envelope and tucked it deep in her coat pocket.

Bonnie nodded. Tears ran down her cheeks.

'My mam,' she said.

'What does she say?'

'Shall I read it to you?'

Bonnie took out the letter again and in a shaky voice began to read aloud.

Ish leaned forward to listen.

She held up the map for him to see. The boat bobbed gently on the dark water.

'Is good,' he said softly. 'Is OK, Bonnie. We find her.'

He picked up the oars again. The boat moved on.

Bonnie's heart was full of pain, and sadness, and a kind of yearning, for the mother she had lost, and almost forgotten. *Almost*. And now there was a new feeling, like a tiny candle flame that strengthens and grows as you shelter it with the palm of your hand.

The moon rose higher, silver and beautiful.

The night seemed to lift, to expand. The sky was a vast canopy of stars and planets around them. Space. Infinite distances.

And they were on their way. They just had to keep moving forward.

That is all we can ever do.

Ish began to sing.

Shalom shalom may peace be with you . . .

Bonnie joined in.

Their voices were thin and tiny, mere specks of sound in the middle of the ocean, the whole vast universe. But that didn't matter. They sang together, and they were moving forward, rowing out towards the shipping channel that would lead them to a safe harbour, and Bonnie's mam, and their new and better life.

Afterword

Imagine this.

It's evening, late spring. Outside a wooden house with blue painted windows and doors, a family of five sits together around a rough wooden table under apple trees.

Ish draws in a large notebook, filling the pages with colour. He brushes away the white petals drifting down from the apple blossom.

'What are you drawing this time?' Mattie peers over Ish's shoulder at the open page. He's a boy of about eleven, with Bonnie's dark hair and Aidan's blue eyes.

'All this!' Ish sweeps his arm wide, as if to include the house and the forest and the lake and all of them.

Bonnie looks from one shining face to another.

Mattie, her new-found brother. Ish, her dearest friend and almost-brother. Aidan and Mam.

Mam smiles back at her. She reaches out and takes Bonnie's hand in her own and squeezes it tight. 'Happy?'

Bonnie nods, her heart too full for words.

A golden moon rises above the lake. Swallows and house martins dip and dive for flies above the still water. The larch forest is alive with birdsong. The tiny firecrests are like bursts of flame among the soft green branches.

In the gathering dusk, the house seems to be full of light.

It shines from every window.

It floods through the open door.

Acknowledgements

Thank you to Bath Spa University for research time to write this book, and to Lucy Christopher for leading the MA Writing for Young People while I was away.

Thank you to my editor Liz Cross, my agent Jodie Hodges, to everyone at Oxford University Press, and to Helen Crawford-White for the beautiful cover image.

About the Author

Julia Green is the author of more than eighteen books for young people. She writes about islands and oceans, the relationship between young people and the natural world, friendship, family, love, loss, and adventure. Julia was born in Ashtead, Surrey; currently she lives in Bath but spends as much time as she can in wild, remote places. She loves the sea, hilltops, woodlands, and beaches. She has two adventurous grown-up sons.

Julia founded and is Course Director for the renowned MA in Writing for Young People at Bath Spa University, which has launched the careers of many children's writers. She enjoys leading creative writing workshops for children and adults in a variety of settings, including festivals and schools.

You can find out more about Julia on her website
www.julia-green.co.uk
Visit her author page on Facebook **@JuliaGreenAuthor**
Follow her on Twitter **@JGreenAuthor**

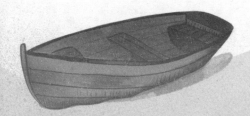

Also by Julia Green